"Are you telling me that you want to *get married? To me?*" Jude laughed incredulously. "That's the most ridiculous thing I've ever heard in my life."

Cesar stiffened. "No child of mine will be born out of wedlock."

"*Born out of wedlock?* Cesar, this is the twenty-first century! In case you hadn't noticed, pregnancy and marriage no longer necessarily go together! Why would you ask me to marry you?"

"Isn't it obvious?" He frowned. He was doing the honorable thing—the *only* thing.

"It isn't just about the child," he told her roughly. "I...I still want you...."

"But I may not want *you*...."

He curled his fingers into her hair and pulled her toward him.

"Shall we put that to the test...?"

Dear Reader,

Harlequin Presents® is all about passion, power, seduction, oodles of wealth and abundant glamour. This is the series of the rich and the superrich. Private jets, luxury cars and international settings that range from the wildly exotic to the bright lights of the big city! We want to whisk you away to the far corners of the globe and allow you to escape and indulge in a unique world of unforgettable men and passionate romances. There is only one Harlequin Presents®, available all month long. And we promise you the world....

As if this weren't enough, there's more! More of what you love. Two weeks after the Presents® titles hit the shelves, four Presents® Extra titles join them! Presents® Extra is selected especially for you—your favorite authors and much-loved themes have been handpicked to create exclusive collections for your reading pleasure. Now there's another excuse to indulge! Midmonth, there's always a new collection to treasure—you won't want to miss out.

Harlequin Presents®—still the original and the best!

Best wishes,

The Editors

Cathy Williams

RUTHLESS TYCOON, INEXPERIENCED MISTRESS

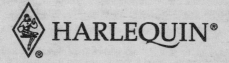

HARLEQUIN®

TORONTO • NEW YORK • LONDON
AMSTERDAM • PARIS • SYDNEY • HAMBURG
STOCKHOLM • ATHENS • TOKYO • MILAN • MADRID
PRAGUE • WARSAW • BUDAPEST • AUCKLAND

Recycling programs
for this product may
not exist in your area.

ISBN-13: 978-0-373-12828-0

RUTHLESS TYCOON, INEXPERIENCED MISTRESS

First North American Publication 2009.

www.eHarlequin.com

Printed in U.S.A.

All about the author…
Cathy Williams

CATHY WILLIAMS was born in the West Indies and has been writing Harlequin® romances for some fifteen years. She is a great believer in the power of perseverance, as she had never written anything before (apart from school essays a lifetime ago!), and from the starting point of zero has now fulfilled her ambition to pursue this most enjoyable of careers. She would encourage any would-be writer to have faith and go for it!

She lives in the beautiful Warwickshire, U.K., countryside with her husband and three children, Charlotte, Olivia and Emma. When not writing she is hard-pressed to find a moment's free time in between the millions of household chores, not to mention being a one-woman taxi service for her daughters' never-ending social lives.

She derives inspiration from the hot, lazy, tropical island of Trinidad (where she was born), from the peaceful countryside of middle England and, of course, from her many friends, who are a rich source of plots and are particularly garrulous when it comes to describing Harlequin® heroes. It would seem, from their complaints, that tall, dark and charismatic men are way too few and far between! Her hope is to continue writing romance fiction and providing those eternal tales of the sort of love for which, she feels, we all strive.

CHAPTER ONE

CESAR was not in the best of moods as he swung his Bentley down the small street into which his sat nav had guided him. It was a little after nine in the evening and the weather, which had looked promising in London for taking his car out for a run, had become increasingly poor the farther east he had travelled. Flurries of snow had kept his wipers busy for the past forty-five minutes.

When he had arranged a meeting with his brother, this venue was not what he had had in mind. In fact, his club in London had been his preferred choice, but Fernando had insisted on meeting in his God-forsaken stamping ground of Kent, a place which held no interest for Cesar and therefore one which he had never seen the need to visit.

He now cursed under his breath as he pulled up in front of a building that had all the charm of a disused warehouse. For a few seconds after he had killed the engine, he stared at what looked suspiciously like graffiti on the walls and wondered whether his faith in computer technology had been misplaced. Had that disembodied female voice which had guided him away from the city centre got the directions all wrong?

With a sharp, impatient click of his tongue, Cesar swung himself out of his car in search of a door of sorts.

He would personally donate his car to the nearest vagrant if his brother lived in this dump. Fernando was not the sort of guy who *did dumps*. In fact, Fernando was the sort of guy who specialised in avoiding them at all costs.

Cesar did his best to swallow his anger at having to deal with this massive personal inconvenience. He was here for a specific purpose and, to that end, there was no point in dwelling on the fact that his Friday night had been ruined. Nor was there any point in getting annoyed with his brother. By the end of the night Fernando would have enough to deal with, never mind his lack of foresight in arranging this meeting, in the dead of winter, miles away from civilisation.

The door was cunningly concealed amidst the graffiti and, for a few seconds after he had pushed it open, Cesar took time to adjust to his surroundings.

This wasn't what he had expected. Disused from the outside the place might well appear to be, but once inside, the picture was vastly different. A few dozen people were milling about what seemed to be a club of sorts. To one side of the semi-darkened room, a cluster of leather chairs and sofas were scattered around low tables. Elsewhere people stood drinking by a long, sleek bar which curved in a U shape to encompass most of the back of the room. To the left there appeared to be a raised podium and yet more chairs.

It didn't take long to spot his brother, talking in a small group, animated as he usually was and the centre of attention.

Having specifically told Fernando that he wanted to have a one-on-one meeting to discuss the small matter of his trust fund, Cesar was enraged to now discover that he had been conned into attending what looked like a private party. The subdued lighting didn't give him much of a clue as to the nature of the guests involved, but he didn't have to exert his brain too much to work out that they would all be his brother's usual cronies. Blonde bimbos, gambling partners and general wastrels who shared the same ambitions as Fernando to spend the family money as flamboyantly as possible whilst simultaneously dodging anything that smelled remotely like hard work.

Cesar grimly thought that his brother was on the wrong track if he thought he could avoid discussing his financial future by conniving to have a bunch of chaperons around him.

By the time he descended on Freddy, all of the group bar one had departed and Cesar treated his brother to a smile of pure displeasure. He didn't bother to look at the crop-haired youth standing next to him.

'Fernando,' he said through gritted teeth. He held out one hand, his cursory nod to courtesy. 'This is not what I expected.' It had been several months since he had laid eyes on his brother. In fact, the last time had been at a family gathering in Madrid, where yet again Cesar's attempts to interest his brother in the fortunes of the company had met with a resounding lack of interest. It was then that he had told Fernando in no uncertain terms that he would be putting his trust fund under the microscope. It was within his power to defer it until such time as he considered it wise to release it and he wouldn't hesitate to use his power of attorney. 'Get your act together,' he had warned, 'or kiss sweet goodbye to that lifestyle of yours.'

Of course, Fernando had responded by staying as far away from the company head office as he physically could.

'I thought…Friday night…' Freddy's smile was pure charm. 'Live a little, big brother! We can talk tomorrow. Actually, I wanted to show you…' He spread his hands in a gesture to encompass the room and Cesar looked at him in cool silence. 'But I am being rude.' He turned to the woman he'd been talking to who had been displaced by Cesar striding in front of her. 'This is Judith—Jude—meet my brother, Cesar… What can I get you, Cesar?' He edged away. 'Whisky? As usual?'

'And I'll have another glass of wine, Freddy.' Jude had to take a few sideways steps until she was standing directly in front of the most intimidating man she had ever set eyes on in her life.

So this was the famous Cesar. No wonder Freddy had been quaking in his proverbial boots at the prospect of having a meeting with him. He was a good four inches taller than his brother and where Freddy was good-looking in an approachable, flirtatious kind of way, this man was stunning. His face was dark and lean and, with its perfect bone structure, somehow forbidding. This was a face that could chill to the bone.

She did her best to smile. This elaborate set-up had been meticulous in the planning. Freddy had been so desperate to introduce his brother to the place he had bought. It was a converted warehouse which was halfway to becoming the sexy jazz club of his dreams, waiting only for the injection of cash from the trust fund which, he had told her worriedly, was in danger of being wrenched away before he could get his hands on a single penny of it. He had invested heavily in the place but it would get no further without Cesar's approval.

How better to get his brother's backing than to entice him into it, show him *what it could be*, prove to him that he was no longer the layabout playboy kid brother he had always been. He had invited all the right people to help him create the perfect setting, including her. Bankers were there, lawyers, a couple of accountants, everybody who had had any input in his burgeoning venture.

'Freddy's told me a lot about you.' She was wearing her flats and had to crane her neck to look up at him.

'Well, I have no idea who you are, nor do I know why Fernando has arranged to meet me here.' He frowned at the girl standing in front of him. He had barely noticed her and he knew why. With her short dark hair, she hardly oozed femininity.

Inherently Spanish, Cesar had a very clear image of what a woman should look like and this wasn't it.

'Do you?' he asked coolly.

'I think he wanted you to meet…some of his friends…'

'I've met Freddy's friends in the past. Believe me when I tell you that I have no desire to meet any more.' That said, he hadn't met *this particular one* before and she certainly wasn't the sort his brother usually went for. In fact, just the opposite. So what was she doing here? He looked at her narrowly, his shrewd brain coming up with possibilities and playing with them. 'Who are you, anyway? And how do you know Fernando? He's never mentioned your name to me in the past.' His brother had a lavish lifestyle and was cavalier with his money. Cesar knew because he had access to all Fernando's bills. He also knew that his brother was fond of spending money on his women. From the age of eighteen, the boy had been a magnet for gold-diggers. This one didn't have the outward appearance of a gold-digger, but Cesar was suddenly keenly interested in finding out what her connection was to his brother. He looked across the room to where the clutch of sofas was being studiously ignored by people who seemed to prefer standing. In a minute Fernando would return with drinks and Cesar was pretty sure a round of boring and pointless introductions would then commence. With his suspicions suddenly roused, he nodded curtly to the sofas.

'I've had a hell of a long trip here. Let's sit and you can tell me…all about your relationship with my brother.'

Jude wondered how an invitation to converse could sound like a threat. Having disappeared in the direction of the bar, Freddy had obviously been waylaid. This was one of Freddy's bad habits. He was capable of striking up a conversation and getting lost in it until he was forcibly dragged away.

'I don't have a relationship with your brother,' she said as soon as she was sitting on one of the mega-expensive sofas artfully arranged at an angle to the wall. The mood lighting here was even more subdued and Cesar's face was all shadows and angles. She laughed nervously and drained the remainder of her glass. 'I feel as though I'm being interviewed.'

'Do you? I have no idea why. I'm just interested in finding out how you know Fernando. Where did you meet?'

'I'm helping him work…on a project…' Jude's brief had been simply to promote Freddy's new-found gravitas and work with him in convincing his brother that he could make a success of his venture.

'What project?' Cesar frowned. As far as he knew, his brother hadn't been near any projects, at least not since his school days, when they had involved felt-tip pens and maps.

'He might want to tell you that himself,' Jude said vaguely, and he sat forward, leaning towards her with his elbows resting lightly on his thighs. Six foot two inches of pure threat.

'Look, I came here to have a serious talk with Fernando about his future. Instead, I find myself in a bar, surrounded by people I have no desire to meet and now treated to some mysterious nonsense about a project Fernando hasn't mentioned to me. What work, exactly, are you doing on this so-called *project*?'

'I'm not sure I like your tone of voice!'

'And I'm not sure I like whatever game it is you're playing. How long have you known Fernando?'

'Nearly a year.'

'Nearly a year. And how close have you become in that time?'

'Where are you going with this?'

'Let's just say that I may not see a great deal of my brother, but I know the way he operates and long-standing platonic friendships with the opposite sex have never been high on his agenda. He's always liked his women willing, able and bedded. He's also always been predictable in his preferences. Blonde, busty, leggy and lightweight in the brains department. So where do *you* fit in?'

Jude felt outraged colour seep into her cheeks and she took a few deep breaths to gather herself. In the silence, Cesar continued remorselessly, 'If he's spoken to you about me, then you are clearly more than just a *business acquaintance*…' He invested that with thinly veiled scepticism. 'So what exactly, are you, then?'

Saved by the bell. Or rather, saved by Freddy, who appeared with drinks on a tray. Cesar watched her expression of relief. He was taking in everything, from that quick look that passed between them to the way his brother leaned towards her and whispered something in her ear, something to which she shook her head and removed herself just as soon as she feasibly could. He lazily watched her departing back, allowing his eyes to rest briefly on the movement of her rear. She might look like a boy but there was something unconsciously sexy and graceful about the way she walked. He'd get back to her later. Something was going on. He could *feel* it, and he wasn't going to let up until he got to the bottom of it. But, for the moment, he would bide his time.

Watch and wait. A very good motto, he had always maintained and he stuck to it as the predictable round of introductions began and he was treated to a suspiciously *normal* group of people. Where were the bimbos? The pampered young men with their idle, vapid conversation and roving eyes? Disconcertingly, everyone here this evening seemed intent on discussing investments with him.

By the end of the evening he found that he was almost enjoying the mystery.

Outside, the snow was now falling much harder. Amidst the throng of people dashing out to their cars, which were parked in a designated area at the back of the building, unlike his which was skewed at an angle at the front, Cesar spotted Jude wrapping a long scarf around her neck and stuffing her hands into her pockets. The lights had been turned on in the foyer and he could see her properly now. Her short hair was streaked with auburn and her face was not at all boyish. The opposite. Long, dark lashes fringed widely spaced brown eyes and her mouth was full and lush, at odds with the gamine appearance.

Fernando may have always had a soft spot for the obvious but who was to say how a gold-digger could be packaged? The more subtle, in a way, could be all the more deadly.

And there she was again, talking in a fast, low undertone to his brother. Talking about *what*?

'I hadn't planned on staying the night,' Cesar said to his brother, barging in on their conversation, which came to an abrupt halt. He wasn't looking at her but he could feel her eyes on him and mentally he flexed his muscles, intrigued at whatever was stirring beneath the surface.

'Ah.' Freddy smiled apologetically. 'There's an excellent hotel in the city…'

Cesar frowned. 'Don't you have a house locally?'

'Well. Apartment, in actual fact. Pretty small…'

Cesar glanced across at Jude, whose eyes were studiously averted, and his mouth tightened a fraction.

'It's snowing pretty heavily,' Cesar said bluntly, 'and I have no intention of driving around in circles looking for somewhere to stay. What's the name of the hotel?'

'Name of the hotel…' Freddy glanced quickly at Jude, who sighed in resignation.

'I have a phone book at my place,' she said grudgingly. 'If you drop me home, I can reserve a room for you.'

'Drop you home? How did you get here?'

'I came with Freddy.'

'Did you now…' Cesar murmured. He smiled and inclined his head to one side. 'Well, that sounds like an offer I'm in no position to refuse… And tomorrow, Fernando…we need to have a little chat…'

'Of course, big brother!' He slapped him warmly on the back and gave him a semblance of a hug, which came naturally to neither of them.

Cesar, accustomed as he was to a stilted relationship with his brother, nevertheless felt a twinge of genuine regret at the lack of real warmth between them. The loss of their parents when he had only just been out of his teens should have brought them closer together. Instead, it had done the opposite. With the mantle of the family's empire resting heavily on his shoulders, Cesar wondered if he had failed in his main duty as a brother—to love him. He had had to don his responsibilities quickly and he had been impatient with Freddy's lack of ambition which he had seen as weakness. He shoved aside the irksome thoughts—he'd worked hard to provide a stable and secure life for his brother. He'd done his best.

'My car's out at the front.'

'Why didn't you use the car park at the rear?'

'Because, believe it or not, I was inclined to think I had arrived at the wrong address when I got here. I never suspected that the place was functional or that there was a parking area at the back.'

Freddy beamed. 'Clever, isn't it? We can discuss all of that tomorrow.' He was already backing away and Jude eyed Cesar warily. The last thing she wanted was to be cooped up in a car with him, go back to her house with him, but she had no choice. Freddy couldn't possibly take him back to the apartment—not with Imogen there.

Just thinking of that little secret by omission made her flush guiltily. Imogen should have been at the little party tonight. She was, after all, the key player in the game, but Freddy had insisted that she be kept out of sight. At least for the moment. Having met Cesar, Jude could understand why, because Cesar was a man in whom suspicion was deeply embedded. She could sense it in his conversation, which had been a thin cover-up for a cross examination. One look at Imogen, her long blonde hair, her big blue eyes and her legs that went on for ever, and Freddy's trust fund would have been written off for good. The fact that she was nearly seven months pregnant with Freddy's baby would have brought on cardiac arrest.

'We could just drive into the city,' Jude said once inside the car, which was as comfortable as any of those wildly overpriced sofas Freddy had insisted on buying for the club. She glanced worriedly at the snow, which was falling thickly white. 'I don't live a million miles from here but my place is down some narrow country lanes and this car might not make it.'

'This car,' Cesar informed her, reversing and swinging the car in the right direction, 'is equipped to cope with anything.'

'Anything except snow in Kent in the middle of January. For that, you really need something a bit more robust. These sorts of fashion cars might be all right for London but they're rubbish out in the country.'

Cesar gave her a look of pure incredulity but she was frowning out of the window, busily trying to work out how fast he could reasonably travel without ending up in a ditch.

She directed him out to the main street which, at a little past one in the morning with the snow pelting down, was deserted. It took a ridiculously long time to clear the city, then came a series of winding country lanes, each one more treacherous than the last.

'How the hell do you make out in these sorts of conditions?' Cesar muttered under his breath, every ounce of concentration focused on getting them to her house in one piece.

'I have a four-wheel drive,' Jude admitted. 'It's old but it's pretty reliable and it can get through just about anything.'

'As opposed to this fashion statement I drive.' He glanced over at her, then back at the road.

'I could never afford a car like this in a million years. Not that I'd ever want one. I don't see the point of them.'

'It's called comfort.' Cesar realised that he didn't know the first thing about her. What job did she have? Aside from helping his brother on some so-called *project*, which could be anything from doing his accounts to colour coordinating his wardrobe. He would need to find out more about her to ascertain what her motives were. For the moment, however, he was too preoccupied with controlling his car in these conditions for too much detailed questioning and, as he rounded a corner at a snail's pace, he began to wonder how he was going to find his way back into the civilised roads of the city and the comfort of a hotel room.

'I would choose practicality over comfort any day of the week.'

'I gathered as much from your choice of clothing tonight.'

'Meaning what?'

'Meaning—is your house going to be coming into view any time soon because, if I go any slower, we might just as well get out of the car and walk the remainder of the way.'

'It's just up ahead.' She pointed to a dim light, barely visible through the downfall, but she was mentally chewing over what he had said about her clothing. Yes, she had worn her jeans because they were comfortable and it hadn't been a fussy affair. She hadn't been the only one there wearing jeans. So maybe most of the women had worn something slightly more formal, but she had looked presentable enough!

She glanced down at her thick black duffel coat and her black boots, which were perfect winter garb although they did seem a little incongruous against the cream luxury leather of his car. Then she slid her eyes across to where he was frowning in concentration at what was trying to pass for a road.

He might be the rudest man she had ever met, but there was no denying that he was frighteningly good-looking. In a scary way, she amended. Not her type at all. He made the hairs on the back of her neck stand on end.

As the car tackled the last lap of the trip, she heard the squeal of tyres and then...nothing.

Cesar swore under his breath and glared at her.

'It's not *my* fault!' she protested immediately.

'How the hell would you have made your way back here? On foot?'

'I would have...' she stopped in the nick of time from telling him that she would have stayed at Freddy's apartment, which would have involved no narrow snow-ridden country lanes, as it was in the city centre—if he couldn't accommodate his own brother, then how could he have possibly accommodated *her*? '...stayed at Sophie's place,' she said quickly, thinking on her feet.

'Damn car!' He scowled and flung open his car door to a sheet of white. 'We'll have to walk the rest of the way.'

'You can't just leave your car here!'

'And you suggest...?'

'I suppose we could try pushing it.'

'Are you completely mad?' He began walking in the direction of the light and Jude half ran to keep up with him. 'I'll have to return for it as soon as the weather shows some sign of clearing.'

'But that might not be for hours yet!' It was occurring to her what that meant and she didn't like it. 'You've got to get to a hotel!'

'Well, why don't you wave a magic wand and maybe the weather will oblige us both by stopping...*this*!' In retrospect, he should have insisted on Fernando travelling to London to see him. In retrospect, he should have stopped at the first sign of snow because he could not afford the luxury of being snowbound *anywhere*. Even on a Saturday, he had vital conference calls to make and meetings to arrange via e-mail with people on the other side of the world. Fernando might be able to lie in when the weather looked a little challenging, but not so for Cesar! He ground his teeth in frustration and raked his fingers through his hair which, in the brief amount of time it had taken them to reach her front door, was already dripping from the snow.

At least the house was warm. Or rather cottage because, from what he could discern in the inky blackness, it was small, white and with a picture-postcard picket fence. Inside was as quaintly pretty, with old wooden floors and a feeling of age and comfort. In short, it was a million miles away from his marvel of pale marble, pale leather and abstract paintings—investments which had cost an arm and a leg.

'Phone book...phone book...' Jude was muttering to

herself as she looked under tables and behind chairs. 'Ah. Here we go. Right. Hotel. Any in particular?'

'Forget it.'

'What do you mean, *forget it*?'

'Look outside.' He nodded in the direction of the window and Jude followed his gaze with a sinking heart. This was turning into a blizzard. He would need a snowplough to clear the roads for his car and a tractor to transport him to the city centre. Other than that, it was madness to even think about leaving the house.

'But you can't stay here!'

'Why not?' Cesar looked at her narrowly, weighing up whether to pursue his line of thought or leave it until the following morning considering the lateness of the hour. 'Would Fernando object?'

'Freddy? Object? Why on earth would he object?' They were both in the small hallway and she felt as though her breath was being sucked out of her. He was so *tall*! He was also removing his coat and she gave a little squeal of horror. Chatting pleasantly to the man for half an hour and singing Freddy's praises was all well and good but enforced overnight companionship was a completely different matter. 'You can borrow my car to get into town!' Pure genius. 'The comfort level's a bit low but you'll make it there in one piece, at any rate, and a hotel would be a lot more comfortable than the floor here…'

'Floor?'

'I know. Appalling.' He was now hanging his coat on the banister and she wanted to fling it back at him, demand that he put it on and send him firmly on his way. 'Small house.' She pointedly kept her duffel coat on so that he would get the message.

'Forget about trying to shove me outside, Jude. I'll leave in the morning and if I have to sleep on the floor, then so be it. I'm certainly not going to risk my life in your clapped-out car in this weather.'

'Oh, very well,' she snapped, edging back a few inches as he stepped towards her.

'So why don't you take your coat off and show me which particular part of the floor you want to designate to me?'

'There's a guest bedroom,' Jude admitted grudgingly, 'but it's very small and very cluttered. You'd find it a very challenging space to sleep in.'

Cesar strolled past her towards the general area of the kitchen, inspecting the surroundings as he went. No signs of his brother in the house, at any rate. At least no photos, no bits of male paraphernalia which, in his brother's case, would probably have been hugely expensive, garishly coloured jumpers or any one of those ridiculous hats which he collected. In fact, no signs of any male occupancy at all.

'Would you like a guided tour?' Jude asked acidly, arms folded. 'Or are you happy just nosing around on your own?'

Cesar turned to her and gave her a long, leisurely appraisal. Not only was she *not* his brother's usual trademark busty blonde, she was also *not* the usual trademark giggly airhead. He really would have to work on finding out just what her job was and how it involved his brother. Maybe the weather could work to his advantage, he thought. Trapped in the confines of her own house, she could hardly disappear if the questions got tough. He smiled slowly, relishing the prospect of asserting his authority and letting her know, in no uncertain terms, that he was not a man to be messed with.

'No,' he said lazily, eyes back on her mutinous, flushed

face. 'The guided tour won't be necessary. At least not at this hour of the morning.'

'Fine. Then, if you follow me, I'll show you where you can spend the night.' Up the stairs, which creaked protestingly under his weight, and to the left, pausing only so that Jude could yank a sheet and a blanket from the airing cupboard. 'I'm sure you know how to make a bed,' she told him, handing over the linen. She was pretty sure he didn't. Like Fernando, he would have been spared the necessity of doing any menial tasks thanks to a background that had seen him raised with all the help that money could buy. It was only after he had met Imogen that he had discovered that *fast food* wasn't just a pre-theatre dinner. She was reliably informed by her friend that he could complete most household tasks now but with record slowness and only dubious success.

She would have liked to have witnessed his botched attempts at bed-making, but she let him get on with it while she swept aside all her stuff and, by the time she looked around, the bed was perfectly made and he was looking at her with an amused smile.

'Up to your standards?' he asked, raising his eyebrows, and she had the grace to blush.

'The bathroom's next door and we share it, so if I'm in it then you'll just have to wait your turn.' She was suddenly flustered as he reached for the top button of his shirt. 'I'll make sure that there's a towel for you.' She backed towards the door as a sliver of hard, muscled, bronzed torso was revealed.

'What's with all the drawings?'

Her mouth went dry as he reached the final button and began to undo his cuffs.

'Are you an artist?' He walked across to the pile of sketches which she had dumped on the ancient pine table, which had begun life as a dressing table but was now used as a surface on which any and everything found its way.

Jude snatched her drawing from his hand and returned it to its place. 'I'm a designer, *actually*.' Thank God she kept all her work in her architect's chest downstairs or he would be rifling through those as well. 'I just do a bit of sketching now and again as a hobby.'

'Well, well, well. *A designer.* Interesting.'

'Yes, it is,' she responded tightly.

'Actually, I meant that it's interesting to discover that you have a proper job. Most of the women who have cluttered up my brother's life have only paid lip service to the work ethic. In fact, the last one to grace my presence was a flightly little thing with a sideline in glamour modelling.'

Jude tried hard not to think of Imogen. What, she wondered with an inward shudder, would he have thought of a *stripper*? She and Imogen went back all the way to pigtails and hopscotch. A couple of poor choices on the boyfriend front had found her working in a nightclub, saving hard so that she could continue her studies and get the qualifications she needed to become a primary school teacher, but Jude doubted whether the man looking at her now would find an ounce of compassion for that sob story.

He appeared to have read her mind because he continued, musingly, 'Naturally I had to ensure that that particular relationship was stillborn.'

'Why?' Jude asked uncomfortably. Images of her pregnant friend rose in her head. 'There's nothing wrong with glamour modelling…'

'A glamour model and my brother equate to a gold-digger out to fleece a golden goose.'

'That's a very cynical way of thinking…'

'It's called the realities of life. Another reality of life is that I would do anything within my power to ensure that my brother is not taken advantage of. Flings with women are all well and good, just so long as they leave the picture. Any unsuitable ones who try to stick around…would have *me* to contend with…' Always a good idea to lay down one or two ground rules, Cesar thought. She might blush like a teenager and appear to have a face as transparent as glass, but he was savvy enough to know that neither of those two things necessarily added up to a personality as pure as the driven snow.

'Well, thank you for that,' Jude told him coolly. 'It's always illuminating to hear what other people think, even if you don't agree with what they say. Although I'd guess that you don't really give a damn whether people agree with what you have to say or not.'

'Bull's eye!' With a quick, easy movement he stripped off his shirt and tossed it on the ground. 'I'll have to dry these in the morning.' Intriguingly, she looked as though she had never seen a man half naked before.

'You're going to sleep…in the… *What are you going to wear to bed?*'

'What I usually wear.' He looked at her in genuine surprise. 'My birthday suit. It's very comfortable. You should approve.'

Jude thought of him sleeping naked, with only a small bathroom separating their rooms, and felt faint. Of course, this was because she had taken an instant dislike to him and, in fact, disapproved of pretty much everything he had had to say, but the image of that muscular, lithe body flung over her sheets and blankets lodged in her head like a burr.

'I'll get you something!'

'You have men's clothes stashed away in your house?' Cesar's ears pricked up but she didn't say anything. She had backed right out of the door and he waited, thinking, until she reappeared two minutes later and tossed him a T-shirt. It was big all right. It was also bright pink.

He could hear the laughter in her voice as she said, 'That should fit. Have a good night's sleep!'

CHAPTER TWO

AT SIX-THIRTY the following morning, the snow had stopped but outside was a landscape of pure wintry white. Very attractive for a postcard, Jude thought sourly, but not so handy when it came with her house guest, the thought of whom had kept her tossing and turning throughout the night. He should never have mentioned that he slept naked. The minute he had told her that, the image of him without his clothes had lodged in her head and all her mechanisms for a peaceful night—counting sheep, planning her day, thinking about the projects she had on the go—had been ruined.

Her highly efficient heating system had kicked in over an hour previously and the house was already beautifully warm. It was also beautifully silent.

She crept stealthily out of her bedroom, wondering whether to use the bathroom and then deciding against it just in case her visitor woke up. She had decided overnight that the less contact she had with him, the better. He was disturbing and, much as she loved Freddy and Imogen both, she didn't see why she should have her life disturbed by a virtual stranger. Of course he would surface at some point but before then she could at least snatch a cup of coffee in relative peace.

She crept down the stairs, which didn't creak because she weighed so much less than he did, and expelled one long relieved breath when she was in the safety of her kitchen.

Like everything else in the cottage, it was small but beautifully proportioned, with two beams across the ceiling, an old but serviceable Aga and a much worn kitchen table, which she had bought second hand from a shop which purported to sell antique pine. Freddy's apartment in the city centre was shiny and new and kitted out in a style that could only have been achieved by an interior designer with a limitless budget. She caught herself wondering what his brother's place looked like and immediately stamped on her curiosity.

She was happily pouring hot water into her mug, back to the kitchen door, when an all too familiar voice said from behind, 'Great. I'll have one, too.'

Jude started violently, with the kettle in her hand, and she gave a cry of shock and pain as hot water splashed over her wrist.

Cesar was next to her before she could turn around and give him the full benefit of her annoyance at finding her privacy invaded.

'What have you done?'

'What are you doing down here?' The man looked bright-eyed and bushy-tailed, as though he had been up for hours, and he was back in his trousers and shirt, although he had appropriated one of the baggy old zip-up sweats which she kept on a hook by the front door for those rare moments when her conscience got the better of her and she decided to go to the gym. It drowned her but on him was pulled tight, leaving her in no doubt as to the build of his olive-skinned muscular body.

'Give me your hand.'

'I know what to do.' She turned away, her heart racing at the sight of him, and switched on the cold water, but he was there before her, holding her hand under the tap and then gently patting it dry with one of the tea towels on the Aga.

Jude watched, mesmerised, those long brown fingers against her pale skin, barely able to breathe properly. His clean masculine scent filled her nostrils and made her feel giddy.

'Clumsy, clumsy,' he tutted under his breath and she glared at him.

'You gave me the fright of my life,' she accused. 'I didn't expect you to be sneaking around at this hour in the morning! You're a guest! Guests stay in bed until they think it's appropriate to emerge!'

'I'm a morning person. Up with the lark, so to speak.' He guided her towards a chair and sat her down. 'Do you have any antiseptic cream? Bandage?'

'I'll be fine as soon as you give me back my hand.'

'Nonsense. As you said, this is my fault.'

Jude couldn't disagree with that. She told him where to find her first aid kit and watched in silence as he efficiently bandaged her hand, treating her with a great deal more concern than the scalding warranted. Much to her discomfort because halfway through the procedure, and having recovered from the shock at having him sneak up on her from behind, she became acutely aware of what she was wearing. A baggy T-shirt, along the lines of the one she had tossed at him earlier on. It reached mid-thigh but thereafter she was fully exposed and all too aware of the unprepossessing image she presented to a man who obviously didn't do casual, judging from his remark about her jeans outfit the night before.

She hunched forward in an attempt to conceal the jutting peaks of her breasts and then realised that she was thereby exposing them to an overhead view so she sat up and glared at his dark head as he put the finishing touch to the bandage.

'Now stay right there and I'll finish what you started.'

'What have you been getting up to down here? How long have you been up?'

'Oh, I only managed to grab a couple of hours' sleep,' Cesar said, his back to her as he made them both a mug of coffee. 'Perhaps it was the novel experience of sleeping in a pink T-shirt.'

Jude took some comfort in imagining him looking ridiculous. Had he been wearing it right now, she figured she might have coped with him being in her space without her body feeling as though it were on fire.

'Then—' he placed her mug of coffee next to her on the table and sat down '—I tried to get the Internet working but it refused to oblige.'

'Phone lines might be down,' Jude said glumly. 'A heavy fall of snow can sometimes do that. It can also be a bit quirky at times.'

A bit like its owner, Cesar thought. He had had time to think things over and had come to the conclusion that nothing would be gained from browbeating her. She was clearly as stubborn as a mule and, from what he could see, given to baring her claws. Far better to put away his armoury and use weapons of a different nature to find out what exactly her role was in his brother's life.

'I then decided to use my time profitably so I went to check on the car.'

'And you got it started?'

'Started but nowhere to go with it. Snow's pretty deep.'

'Couldn't you have scraped the snow away? You're a strong man,' she added boldly. 'Men do stuff like that.'

'Sure, if I'd wanted to spend the next eight hours outside in the freezing cold—and here's some more bad news. The sky looks grim and the weather reports are talking about more snow in the next twenty-four hours.'

'They can't be!' Jude all but wailed.

'Hazard of living in this part of the world. I can count on the fingers of one hand the number of times I've seen snow in London.'

'How can you be so…so *calm* about all of this?'

'Why get hot and bothered about something over which I have no control?' Sure, he had uttered a few ungentlemanly curses when he had discovered the lack of Internet connection but he had now resigned himself to the fact that the business world would have to spend at least part of the weekend without him. For Cesar, this was no small thing. Work was his driving force. It took precedence over everything and everyone.

'Because you live for your work! You practically have a bed in your office!'

'And how do you know that?'

'Freddy told me.' It had slipped out before she had time to catch it and Jude shot him a sheepish look. He might rub her up the wrong way but she knew that she would have hated the thought of being discussed behind her back. 'He just mentioned it in passing,' she amended.

'You two seem to share quite a close relationship…considering it's purely professional…'

'I never said that it was *purely professional*…'

'But you told me that you were working on a project with him.'

'I am. Was. Am.'

'Past tense? Present tense? Which is it to be? And you never said precisely what this so-called project is.'

'I told you, that's something I know Freddy would want to

tell you about himself.' She belatedly remembered that she was supposed to support him whenever and wherever possible. 'And it's very exciting.'

'Well, I can't wait to find out what it's all about. I'm literally on the edge of my seat. If my little brother is involved, then it's sure to be a non-starter. His business sense has always been fairly non-existent.' He finished his coffee and pulled out a stool so that he could prop both feet up—something, she noted, he seemed quite at ease doing considering he was in someone else's house. 'So he told you that I'm his workaholic brother, did he? In between discussing his mystery project?'

'You make it sound as though it's a crime to be friends with Freddy.'

Cesar decided not to inform her that it would only be a crime should she want to adjust her position from *friend* to *spouse*.

'I'm just curious. Project to friend? Friend to project? What was the order of events? How did you meet?'

Jude looked at him warily. That earnest expression on his face didn't fool her a bit. He was taking small steps around her, looking for clues.

'I'm a designer,' she mumbled, trying to sort out how she could avoid divulging details about their meeting, which had happened courtesy of Imogen. 'And he needed some stuff doing…'

'Oh, yes. The stuff he wants to talk to me about. And, at that point, did you know how much Fernando was worth?'

'I knew that's where all your questions were leading!'

'I'm that obvious?' Cesar asked indifferently.

'Yes, you're *that* obvious, not that you care! I have to go and get changed.' She stood up and gave him a withering look, which had zero effect. He still carried on calmly looking at her, as though he had all the time in the world to wait until she decided to deliver the answer he wanted to hear.

'Please don't bother on my account,' Cesar drawled, taking in the shapely legs which had been disguised the night before in their jeans. For someone with dark hair and dark eyes, she was delicately pale and her skin was like satin. He had become used to a diet of women who slapped on make-up. Jude, he absent-mindedly noticed, was wearing none and her face was fresh and smooth. She had a sprinkling of freckles across her nose and he imagined that she might have been a tomboy, climbing trees and doing everything the boys did.

Jade ignored him. 'I haven't been eyeing up your brother as marriage material so that I can get my hands on his fortune,' she said tightly. 'And it's totally out of order for you to repay my hospitality by insulting me!'

'Come again?'

'I could have…left you to find your way round Canterbury in the snow so that you could source a hotel!' Theoretically. He wasn't to know that the pleading look Freddy had given her had warned her that he needed help just in case Cesar found himself programming his sat nav for his brother's apartment—a very strong possibility considering his lack of familiarity with the city and the deteriorating weather. Okay, so maybe *hospitality* implied more than had actually been delivered, because *hospitality* implied a smiling welcome, but she was sticking to her guns. 'You could have ended up lost and trapped in that silly car of yours.'

'*Silly car?*'

Jude made an inarticulate, defiant sound under her breath and glared at him. 'I'm not a gold-digger. I'm not even materialistic! I don't believe that money can buy happiness. The opposite, in fact! I've worked with loads of really rich people who have been miserable as anything. *In fact*,' she tacked on meaningfully, 'are *you* happy because you work all the hours God made so that you can accumulate more money than anyone could possibly spend in a lifetime? Freddy says that you bury yourself in your work because you've never really recovered from…' She went bright red and covered her treacherous mouth with her hand.

'From *what*…?' Cesar asked softly.

'Nothing.'

'What did my brother say?'

'I really need to go and change now!' She fled. She didn't understand how she could have been so thoughtless, just lashing out at him because he had accused her of being a gold-digger. What he'd said meant nothing to her. She should have been able to hear him out and shrug it all off because whatever he thought was never going to be her problem. Instead…

She locked the bathroom door and leaned against it for a few seconds with her eyes closed, before turning on the shower and taking her time under the cascading water.

She felt better once she had showered and even better when she had jettisoned her silly nightie in favour of her favorite fitted jeans and a tight long-sleeved T-shirt. For some indefinable reason she defiantly wanted to show Cesar that she at least had a figure of sorts!

The smell of bacon sizzling greeted her halfway down the stairs and her stomach churned in immediate response. If this was Cesar at the stove, then he was clearly more domesticated than she'd thought he'd be, imagining this brooding billionaire to be the type who had never knowingly sought out any culinary device. She walked into the kitchen and watched for a few silent seconds as Cesar popped some bread in the toaster and then began to beat eggs in a bowl.

'You ran away before you could tell me what other little gems Fernando has shared with you,' Cesar said without turning around.

'I'm sorry.' Jude took a deep breath and went to sit at the table. She stared at the bandage, then looked at Cesar's aristocratic profile. His face was a lesson in beauty, his features sharply, powerfully defined. A portrait artist would have given their right arm to paint him. He had rolled his shirtsleeves to the elbows. His hands were sinewy and strong and she looked away quickly. 'I told you that you were out of order to insult me in my own home and I was out of order to bring up something which is none of my business. Can we call it quits? Maybe start arguing about something else?'

'I take it he told you about Marisol,' Cesar said flatly. He had never found himself in the position of talking about his private life before, even though his late wife was not exactly a subject that was out of bounds. Hell, check his profile on the Internet and up the information would come.

'I'm very sorry.'

'For what? For not, as he insinuated, recovering from her death?' He leaned against the counter and met her gaze coolly, steadily.

'Like I said, it's none of my business.'

'You're right. It's not, but if you want to make it your business, then feel free to look it up when your Internet connection's been restored.' Had he never recovered? Was that the general consensus whispered behind his back? No one had ever dared say anything like that to his face, not even his uncle in Madrid, to whom he was close. The thought of other people having opinions on his state of mind made his mouth tighten in anger but there was no point in venting any of that anger on the woman sitting opposite him. He never allowed other people's opinions to have an effect on him and he wasn't going to start now.

Briefly, though, he thought about his late wife, Marisol. She had been dainty and, peculiarly for a Spanish girl, fair. Cesar, just eighteen at the time, had taken one look at her and had known, in that instant, that he had to have her. It had been a union blessed by both sets of parents and Marisol, for that brief window when she had been alive, had lived up to every expectation. She had been the sweetest woman he'd ever met. She had cooked amazing meals, had not once complained at the hours he kept. She had been a woman born to be protected, looked after, sheltered and he had been more than happy to oblige. What man wouldn't, for a soothing domestic life?

And since Marisol, although he had never contemplated a replacement, he had always been attracted to the same kind of woman. Unbearably pretty and willing to be at his beck and call. As luck would have it, things usually deteriorated with them when his boredom levels were breached, but that never bothered him. He wasn't in it for the long haul. Did that mean that he *had never recovered*? That he couldn't live life fully after a tragedy that had happened more than ten years ago?

He frowned at the wide brown eyes staring back at him and thought, irritably, that he would have been hard pressed to find a less soothing woman than her. Didn't she know that men weren't attracted to women who approached life like a bull in a china shop? He was fast coming to the conclusion that if his brother *was* involved in any way with the woman, aside from platonically, he was a candidate for the loony-bin.

'And you can stop oozing sympathy,' he grated.

'I'm not *oozing sympathy*. I was just wondering how come you never settled down with someone else.'

'Why haven't *you*?' He returned to his task of making

them something to eat. It was unusual to find him behind a stove and his repertoire of dishes was limited, but he had never taken advantage of the family fortune in the same way that his brother had and consequently was more than capable of fending for himself.

'I believe in kissing a few frogs so that I can recognise the prince when he comes along.'

'And how many frogs have you kissed?'

'I lose count.'

Several kissed frogs but only one who had become close enough for her to be seduced into thinking that he might be *the one*. It had been three years ago and it had ended amicably enough when he had sat her down and gently broken it to her that she wasn't the woman for him, that he hoped they could remain *friends*. Remaining *friends*, she had later concluded, was just the coward's way of exiting a relationship with the minimum amount of fuss. If a guy didn't want some woman crying all over him then he did that gentle smiley thing and carried on about remaining *friends*, but a let-down was still a let-down and in retrospect Jude could have kicked herself for not at least asking him *why*. Instead, she had stuck out her chin and saved her tears for after he'd gone.

She had no intention of telling any of that to Cesar, however, and she was thankful that he wasn't looking at her because, when he did, he always gave her the impression that he had some kind of weird insight into what was going on in her head.

'That many…'

'Yes, *that many*.'

'And why did none of these frogs turn out to be the prince in disguise?' He put a plate in front of her, brimming with bacon and eggs, far more than she could have eaten in a month of Sundays.

'How is it that you can cook a meal and make a bed and your brother is so hopeless?'

'Is that your not so subtle way of changing the subject?' Cesar sat down, fork in hand, and began tucking into his breakfast, which was roughly double the amount he had set in front of her. 'I find that it pays to be able to do everything for myself, even if I might choose not to, and that includes cooking and cleaning.'

'Fine. In that case you can make yourself useful around here if you can't drive back for a couple of hours...' Jude glanced outside at the unpromising sight of snow flurries, which seemed to be reminding her that the weather forecasters might have had their fingers on the button when they'd predicted more snowfall. 'I'm pretty useless at both.' Their eyes met for an instant and Jude flushed. 'Or at least uninterested.'

Cesar grunted. It was a grunt, Jude decided, that was laced with criticism. She could just *feel* it. The man didn't have to actually *say anything* to make his opinions clear. Poor Freddy, written off by his big brother because he didn't like wearing a suit and going into an office every day to stare at charts and profit and loss columns, having his ideas greeted with those grunts of disapproval.

'I guess you're one of those ultra-traditional men who think that all women should either be chained to a stove or else whistling a merry tune as they push a vacuum cleaner up and down the stairs,' she said tetchily.

'I admit that when it comes to the opposite sex I have pretty traditional views—am I letting myself in for a feminist lecture now? Because you seem to be very sensitive on the subject.'

'Of course I'm not sensitive on the subject,' Jude scoffed, stabbing a piece of bacon with her fork. She thought of James, the disappearing ex-boyfriend who had left smiling and apologising and wittering on about remaining friends. Eight months ago she had heard through a mutual acquaintance that he had since married a sweet blonde thing who had instantly become pregnant and they were both busily doing up a house somewhere in Wiltshire in preparation for the new arrival.

'Most men are...' he said provocatively. 'Fernando included.'

'Is that your way of warning me off him, should I have ideas above my station lurking at the back of my mind?' She stood up, plate in hand, and went across to the sink, from which she had a spectacular view of increasing snow.

When she looked around, it was to find him clearing the rest of the table. In an ideal world he would have remained sitting, she supposed, having enjoyed a lavish breakfast prepared by his woman, who would tidy the kitchen without asking for help and then make him comfortable in the sitting room with a newspaper and a roaring fire. Curiosity reared its unwelcome head again and she caught herself wondering what these women of his looked like. Freddy had told her that he apparently had killer appeal when it came to the opposite sex.

'Maybe—' she smirked '—Freddy isn't quite as traditional as you think.'

Cesar looked at her sharply and Jude shot him a mysterious smile. In actual fact, traditional-hearted Freddy had found his perfect match in Imogen because, never mind her past occupation, she was as conventional and feminine as they came and always had been. Barbie dolls had been her favourite toys at the age of seven, pink her favourite colour at the age of fourteen and she was a dream in the kitchen. While Jude had been playing football with the boys, her best friend had been experimenting with make-up and, for every botched meal Jude had scraped into the rubbish bin in Home Economics class, Imogen had produced its faultless equivalent. And enjoyed it!

'Meaning what?'

'Meaning you don't give your brother enough credit.' Well, that was certainly true enough. She had worked with Freddy from every angle when it came to the jazz club, had heard him explain his ideas lucidly and persuasively to accountants, had seen his fledgling plans slowly come to fruition without hitches...

'I know Fernando better than you think.' Did he, though? Would Fernando be attracted to a fiery, opinionated, mutinous, downright exasperating woman like this one? A woman who said whatever was on her mind and hang the consequences? Fernando, Cesar thought, would never be able to handle a woman like her! She had said that there was no romantic involvement between them. Was there? It annoyed him that his usual unerring accuracy at reading women seemed to be letting him down now.

'Even though you never see him?' Jude asked sweetly. She began washing the dishes.

'I don't see my brother because I literally don't get the time.' Cesar walked towards the kitchen door, thought better of leaving and turned back to look at her with a disgruntled, exasperated expression. 'Yes, I work damn long hours. When I took over the company, it was in the throes of internal warfare. I stabilised it and hauled it into the twenty-first century, selling off what I had to and sinking money into speculative investments that paid off. None of that gets done sipping cocktails on a beach in the Caribbean or hitting the slopes in Aspen!' He raked his fingers through his hair and glowered at her as she continued to pile the dishes haphazardly on the dish rack. 'I've never known my brother to rise to the challenge of anything,' Cesar heard himself saying. 'And that includes his choice of women.'

'And you do?' Jude turned to look at him. He was leaning against the door frame and the strength of his personality seemed to fill the kitchen, unseen but powerful and suffocating.

His lack of an immediate answer supplied the information she wanted.

'My choice of women is not the issue here.'

'You should give Freddy a chance. He feels…'

'Feels what…? I'm all ears.'

'*Inadequate* compared to you. He feels that you'll shoot him down in flames because he hasn't followed in your footsteps. At the snap of your fingers, his trust fund will go up in smoke and I don't suppose that's the nicest feeling in the world.'

'He's told you all this, has he? Or are these loose interpretations based on a one-year relationship?'

'He's told me.'

'Have you had sex with him?'

'*What?*'

'You heard me. You are clearly sleeping with Fernando, because your conversations seem pretty meaningful.'

'Our conversations are *normal*.' Jude was bright red, her hands clenched at her sides. '*Normal* people discuss how they feel about things, what their hopes and dreams are…' And these had been with Imogen present, just random, casual conversations over spaghetti bolognese at his flat, with some music playing in the background and the three of them all having one too many glasses of wine and putting the world to rights. Cesar might invest something meaningful into her last statement but Jude wasn't going to supply him with a blow-by-blow description of who said what and where and how and when.

'You've vaguely answered part two of my question but what about part one?'

'No, I haven't slept with your brother, not that it's any of your business.'

Cesar looked at her carefully. 'Tell me something... If you're so close to Fernando and you spend hours spilling your hearts out to each other and bonding, why is he so desperate to get his hands on his trust fund at this precise moment in time? He's been more than happy to lead a carefree lifestyle on the allowance he gets for doing no work whatsoever, yet the last time I spoke to him he sounded desperate... Bit of a puzzle, that...'

'His project,' Jude stammered uneasily. And the fact that, while he did indeed get an allowance, he had always funded his lifestyle by sending his bills to Cesar to be paid. Cesar had, through devious means, known pretty much where his money went and could practically track the progress of his relationships by the gifts he had bought for whatever girlfriend he'd happened to be seeing at the time. In short, he had always been accountable. Silk dresses and diamonds, weekend breaks in exotic countries, hotel bills for two—his personal life vetted to a large extent by Cesar, who would step in if he deemed it necessary. Cesar, he had confided in Jude, was very hot on protecting the family fortune from unsuitable women but that had never bothered Freddy because he had never had any intention of getting too wrapped up with anyone. If bills for nursery equipment and baby gear began appearing on the statements, then Cesar would descend with frightening speed and it didn't take a genius to figure out what his reaction would be when he saw Imogen. The trust fund would give him independence.

'If I approve whatever scheme he has in mind, then I would be more than happy to invest in it and set aside the headache of putting Fernando in charge of staggering wealth when he has yet to prove that he would know what to do with it. So did he mention *why* the hurry?'

Jude tried to look as though she might be searching her memory bank for any helpful information on that front, then she shook her head and shrugged. 'I guess he just wants to take control of his life. I mean, he *is* nearly twenty-five...'

'Ancient.'

'*You* were younger than that when you took charge of your empire, or whatever you want to call it.'

'I was responsible.'

'Of course. Silly me. Crazy to think that you might have had a trace of recklessness in your body.'

'If by *reckless* you mean a healthy, active sex life with an interesting variety of women, then, I assure you, you couldn't be further from the truth. If, on the other hand, you mean an ability to squander money on passing pleasures without any thought to the future, then you're spot on. I'll willingly confess to being ridiculously cautious...'

Jude blinked as her active mind hived off on the same unwelcome tangent that had kept her tossing and turning the night before.

Her breasts felt heavy and tender and the brush of her lacy bra over her nipples was almost painful.

'I think...we should think about what we're going to do with the day,' she said hastily, folding her arms squarely in front of her. 'I agree it would be silly for you to try and dig that car of yours out of the snow when there's more falling, but there's no point getting under each other's feet.'

'You should give lessons on how to be the perfect hostess.'

'I've got some work I can be getting on with. In my office. Well, I have a little room off the sitting room that I use as an office, anyway. You can...'

'Make myself scarce?' He pushed himself away from the door frame, his sharp mind tallying their conversation and re-playing it. She had been sincere in her denial that there was anything sexual between herself and Fernando but, that being the case, why her unease the minute his questions became too probing? Why did she behave like a cat on a hot tin roof in his presence?

He looked narrowly at her and the heightened colour in her cheeks, then his eyes drifted to those arms tightly folded over her chest. A very protective gesture, he thought. He knew that he could be intimidating. He liked that. It often helped to keep people at a distance, especially for a man like him, someone at the very pinnacle of his field, which was a situation that en-couraged on the one hand sycophants, on the other predatory sharks who wouldn't hesitate to cosy up to him while clutch-ing knives behind their backs. It also helped as a silent reminder to any woman that, however physically close they got, he was not up for grabs.

Maybe that was it. Maybe she got jittery in his presence and, face it, he was an intruder in her house, snowbound and with zero means of transport out. Or maybe those whispered conversations he had noticed between his brother and her pointed to something going on under the surface, something that made her nervous around him.

Or maybe—and he mulled this last option over with a little kick of satisfaction—just maybe he made her nervous for a perfectly understandable reason. He was a red-blooded man and she, if he wasn't mistaken, was a woman who was all fire where it mattered if only she knew it. Couldn't pretty much everything in life go right back to the elemental?

CHAPTER THREE

IT WAS lunch time before Jude emerged from her office, where she had spent her time redoing her sketches for a loft conversion which, according to the couple who had employed her, had to make them feel as though they were somewhere by the sea. It was a tall order for a Victorian house on the outskirts of a city.

The first thing that greeted her was the sight of Cesar, bare-backed, with a stack of freshly cut logs next to the open fire, which was in full swing.

'Just in case the power goes,' he explained. 'If it can snow like this out here, then anything's possible.'

Jude nodded. The sight of his bare skin flickering in the glow from the open fire seemed flagrantly intimate, although he looked at her innocently enough before walking across to the bay window and nodding at the leaden yellow-grey skies outside, barely visible through the now heavy snowfall. 'The Internet connection's still AWOL so I figured I might as well make myself useful. Manage to get much work done?'

'Work?'

'You've been cooped up in there for four hours!'

She thought of the discarded drawings tossed into the waste-paper bin because her thoughts wouldn't leave her alone. 'Yes. It was very useful.' She made a big effort to stop gaping and actually walked into the sitting room, which was wonderfully warm.

'I've switched off the central heating in the room,' he told her. 'Hope you don't mind.' Cesar had been stared at before. Many times. But never like this, never by a woman who so obviously didn't want to look at him and yet couldn't help herself. It was fiercely erotic. He had, and he hadn't mentioned this, also hand-washed his socks, his boxers and his shirt. At the moment his nakedness against the zipper of his trousers was threatening to need adjustment.

'How did you know where to find the wood?'

'Little shed at the back of the house. Not that tricky, really.' He prodded the fire with the poker, making sure that his back was towards her so that he could give his body time to cool down. Eventually, when he had himself under control, he strolled towards the chair and wiped his face on one of her T-shirts—the very one she had thrown at him the night before.

'Well, thank you. There was no need. The central heating's very efficient in this house. I make sure of that. Shall I get you something to put on? One of my T-shirts?'

'I'm not sure they would fit,' Cesar drawled, 'unless it's one of those baggy ones you seem to like sleeping in.'

Jude refused to be goaded by his remark. Instead, she hurried upstairs and snatched the biggest of her T-shirts out of the chest of drawers because the sooner he covered himself up the better. He obviously hadn't stripped on purpose. He had stripped because chopping logs and starting a fire was a sweat-inducing job, especially once the fire really got going. He wasn't to know that his semi-nudity was just fuelling all sorts of unwanted thoughts in her head. She could swear that her eyesight had gone bionic because she had even been able to make out a trickle of perspiration along his ribcage.

'Well, at least it's not pink,' he said, reaching out and casually brushing her outstretched hand in the process. 'I don't think my male pride could have stood it.'

'Stood what?'

Keep your eyes focused on his face, my girl, and you'll be all right. Definitely don't give in to the temptation to stare at the way his muscles ripple whenever he moves his arms. Or the fact that he has flat brown nipples and a tangle of dark underarm hair.

'Being on public display wearing a girlie colour.'

This was a different Cesar to the grim-faced one who laid down laws and issued threats. This one was smiling at her. A crooked, amused smile that made her toes curl.

'Real men aren't afraid to wear pink,' she said automatically, and Cesar kept her eyes locked to his.

'Trust me. I'm all man.'

'I should go and get us both something to eat. You must be famished after a morning chopping wood. I have some… er…pasta…' she gabbled, taking a step back towards the kitchen. 'I can rustle something up. I'm not great, I have to warn you…but I do a good carbonara…spaghetti…nothing fancy…' The pale blue T-shirt sported a cartoon character but somehow he didn't look silly in it. If anything, it made him more frighteningly masculine, accentuating his biceps and the lean hardness of his stomach.

'Carbonara…spaghetti…nothing fancy…will do just fine, and yes, I'm famished, but I didn't want to start rummaging in your kitchen for food. I know how territorial women can be about men rummaging through their cupboards…I'm surprised you managed to work with your hand bandaged…'

'It doesn't hurt.' She stumbled over her words, instinctively flexing her fingers to prove her point. 'You made a big deal over nothing.'

'Maybe I enjoyed it,' he came back, quick as a flash. 'Don't you know that there's nothing a man finds more appealing than a damsel in distress…?'

'I'm not the damsel in distress type. If you wait *right here* I'll go and fix us lunch.'

She might have guessed, five minutes later, that giving him an order to do something would have the opposite effect because, in his new, confusing good mood, he appeared in the kitchen just as she was fumbling with an onion and debating whether to get rid of the wretched bandage so that she could actually move slightly quicker than a snail.

'Allow me.'

Jude stiffened but didn't look at him as he relieved her of the knife and began expertly peeling and chopping the onion, giving her the far less onerous task of pouring them both a glass of wine because, he told her, it was as dark as night outside and, besides, when did he ever get the chance to consume alcohol at lunch time?

It was a passing remark but it struck him that he very rarely gave himself any chance to really enjoy his leisure time. He had wined and dined many women over the years but courtship was a game he played and the final outcome was already written on the cards before the first meal was even halfway through.

This was different. He might not have been here of his own volition but now that he was, and without the benefit of work as a distraction, he found that he was actually enjoying chopping an onion, frying bacon, playing the domestic man that he never was because his interaction with women never evolved into doing tasks together. He took them to expensive restaurants and sat next to them in theatres and made love to them in his vast bed, but never this.

He saluted her with a raised glass once their concoction was made and nodded to the kitchen table.

'Aren't you a little bored being cooped up here?' she asked tentatively. 'I don't suppose this is what you usually get up to on a weekend.'

'No, it's not.'

'What *do* you get up to?' Curiosity got the better of her and she looked at him over the rim of her glass.

'I work by day and play by night. Occasionally, I skip the play bit if I'm busy.'

'Who do you play with?' Jude blushed, confused to have asked the question but the wine had loosened her tongue, as had his change of attitude. She was no longer on the defensive, wondering where the next barb was coming from, and, released from that constraint, she went beyond her surreptitious appreciation of his masculinity to an even deadlier appreciation of the complex, intelligent, witty *person* behind that formidable, unbearably handsome mask. She began to really see why he was such a killer with the opposite sex. He wasn't being remotely flirtatious and yet there was something indefinably magnetic about him.

She barely noticed how much she was drinking. She was too busy listening to his casual admission that he hadn't, actually, *played* with anybody for the better part of six months. Had she? With the tables neatly turned on her, Jude heard herself ruefully admitting that her playtime stretched a whole lot longer than his. Then, even more surprising because she had never really talked about her ex-boyfriend to anyone, not even to Imogen, who had obviously known the bones of what had happened, she heard herself baring her soul to Cesar.

'So there you are. You were right on one count—men are pretty predictable in the kind of women they go for and it's not the kind of woman *I* am.'

For some reason Cesar felt a spurt of anger towards the unknown stranger who had brought home to her that life was a pretty disillusioning business.

'And stop me now before I get even more maudlin.' Jude laughed and stood up so that she could begin setting the table. 'Too much wine, I'm afraid. One more glass and you'd better watch out. I'll start feeling weepy and sorry for myself.'

'I have very broad shoulders.'

'I know. I'd noticed.'

There was an electric silence. She may have only consumed one glass of wine but not even that slight tipsy, reckless feeling could blind her to the fact that she had just blurted out something horribly private that should have been kept to herself.

And he was looking at her in a very peculiar way.

'When you were…stoking the fire…' she continued lamely, dropping her eyes. At times like these, wouldn't a curtain of long hair have been convenient! She could have hidden behind it. 'I don't often get semi-clad men in my cottage…'

'No, not for a few years, at any rate…'

'I knew I shouldn't have told you that,' Jude said with a hint of bitterness in her voice. She brought the pan over to the table and curtly told him that he could help himself. Guests first and he *had*, after all, cooked it all himself.

'Why do you say that?'

'Say what?'

'That you shouldn't have told me about your ex.'

'Because I don't need you, *or anyone*, being in a position to use information against me at some later date. I don't need anyone to feel sorry for me. I *made a choice* to give myself a break from guys after James and I'm not ashamed of that.' She attacked her food fiercely and glared down at the coil of spaghetti around her fork.

'You really loved this guy, didn't you.'

'I cared about him,' Jude said stiffly. 'I wouldn't have stayed with him for over two years if I hadn't.'

'Stayed with him in the expectation that the relationship would eventually lead to marriage?'

'I suppose.'

'And you never spotted the cracks?'

'I honestly don't want to talk about this.'

'Fair enough. Although….'

It was just one word but it drew her in and she said sullenly, 'Although *what*? I know you're just dying to tell me what's on your mind.'

'We're stuck here.' Cesar shrugged. 'A little conversation passes the time of day and it's not as though I can get through to any of my colleagues. Have you tried the phone? Lines are down. I could always use my mobile…' though the temptation wasn't there, for some reason '…but no charger, so I'm conserving the battery.'

'They're not!' She went over to the phone and then looked at him. 'They are.'

'Yep. Only outside contact I've had is with Fernando to let him know I'm safe and sound and not buried under ten foot of snow somewhere on the outskirts of the city. And you'll be relieved to know that I didn't mention that I had spent the night here. So…no landline, no computer access, limited mobile access—what choice do we have but to make do with each other's company?'

'Is that why you've started to be a bit more pleasant?' It was almost a relief to snipe at him. Just back then—talking to him with the wine flowing through her veins and his smile making her feel all hot and bothered and self-conscious—she had felt like someone walking on the edge of a precipice, with a sharp drop on one side and the comfort of safety on the other.

'I'm intrigued by the irony of someone who is at liberty to psychoanalyse my relationships with women as a response to the death of my wife twelve years ago and yet seems unable to see that her self-imposed exile from emotional involvement with men is her response to a failed relationship.' Cesar forked some food into his mouth and carried on looking at her. 'You're not eating.'

'My appetite seems to have disappeared.'

'Because you're uncomfortable being asked about some guy who led you down the garden path and then dumped you. I'm not the monster you seem to think I am and I'm not laughing at you because you've been celibate for a while.' What he could have added but didn't was that, with no access to the outside world, he now found himself doing something he had never done before. Cesar was taking an interest in a woman beyond the physical. Mostly, his conversations with the opposite sex, unless conducted in the working arena, were laughably superficial. He didn't encourage emotional outpourings.

'Okay, maybe I'm a bit over-cautious when it comes to men, maybe I just don't like getting too close. In fact, your brother is the first guy I've really felt comfortable with for ages,' she admitted and she knew why. Freddy was no threat. He wasn't going to try and pounce on her. He was wrapped up with Imogen and was therefore a safe bet for friendship and it had to be said that having a man as a friend was a huge plus because men brought a different take on all sorts of things. She had forgotten how invaluable they were when it came to putting things into perspective.

'Is that a fact?' Cesar murmured softly, watching the smile on her face.

'I know.' She looked at him, still smiling to herself. 'I know you've had your problems with Freddy, but you'd be surprised at how practical he can be when it counts.'

'Practical…' Well, that, Cesar thought, was a first when it came to recommendations. He stood up and, when she followed suit, told her to go and make herself comfortable in the sitting room. Why waste the fire?

'I should help tidy these things away.'

'You're an invalid.'

'Hardly. Oh, yes, forgot. Damsel in distress.' She glanced down at the bandaged hand with sudden amusement. 'I'm beginning to see that I've played things all wrong. Maybe, instead of trying to be independent, I should have been dropping hankies on the ground and batting my eyelashes so that dashing men would fall at my feet in their eagerness to help me out.'

Cesar was tempted to tell her that he couldn't picture her batting her eyelashes although, when he looked at her, he could see that she had very long eyelashes indeed, eminently suited to playing coy. Where other women enhanced theirs with mascara and eye make-up, for her there was no need.

'Maybe you should,' he said non-committally, but as she disappeared towards the sitting room, leaving him with a sink-load of dirty dishes and the novel experience of washing them, he had plenty more to think about. That faraway, dreamy look in her eyes when she had sung his brother's praises. What did that mean? The random thoughts that had been playing around in his head since the night before now coalesced into something a lot more concrete and a lot more disturbing.

So she hadn't yet slept with Fernando. He was convinced

of that. The woman didn't seem to have the ability to dissemble. He also believed that she had been hiding out from involvement with any man because she had been burnt before.

Where Fernando figured in this jigsaw puzzle was now becoming a little more obvious. He had no one in tow at the moment. Cesar knew that because there had been no charges recently for classy weekend breaks or expensive items of jewellery. For Fernando, whose lifestyle was nothing if not predictable, that could only indicate one thing. He was currently without a woman and, from the looks of it, had been for a while.

Cesar rested both hands flat on the edge of the kitchen sink and gazed thoughtfully at the steadily falling snow.

He had dropped his accusations, had adopted a different approach and, sure enough, he had got what he wanted or at least he had got the pieces he had needed to turn the puzzle into a mathematical equation he could solve.

Jude, reading between the lines, had been in a deep freeze and he didn't know whether her thaw when she met Fernando had been deliberate or whether it had been accidental, but thaw she had. He had seen that in the expression on her face when she had talked about him and heard it in the tone of her voice.

She had given him a load of spiel about not being materialistic but that, he now cynically considered, was something that had to be taken with a huge pinch of salt. People were fond of throwing their hands up in the air and spouting forth about the best things in life being free, but show them a shed-load of cash and the free goodies suddenly didn't seem quite so tempting.

Had she decided somewhere along the way that a friendship, played right, could lead to financial security for the rest of her life?

He thought of her and irritably shrugged off the nagging

unease that her sharp, straightforward, argumentative personality was at odds with the picture he was piecing together. She seemed as keen, in her own way, as Fernando was in getting hold of the precious trust fund. How many times had she mentioned all his brother's marvellous and hitherto unseen virtues of common sense and responsibility? Sure, she might be innocently complimenting him because she was his friend and nothing more. On the other hand, she could be fuelled by motives that were a hell of a lot more suspect.

He ignored the little voice in his head that was telling him that Fernando was a big boy now, well capable of taking care of himself, that he could make his own choices as far as women were concerned and that really, maybe the two of them genuinely had a good thing going and that hell, she was a damn sight better than some of his other catches.

Instead, he focused on the fact that their interaction at that club had not been the interaction of a man and a woman in the throes of a passionate affair after months of mutual teasing. There had been a few whispered conversations, a few furtive looks when they had thought themselves unobserved, but no accidental brushing of bodies and no mysterious disappearances.

So where did that leave him? Was she an out-and-out gold-digger? And, even if she was, was it really any of his business? Hand over the trust fund and walk away. He could do that. Leave Fernando to make a mess of his life in the full understanding that rescue down the line would not be part of the deal. Or withhold the trust fund and protect his brother's financial interests, except at what point would the protection end?

He frowned darkly, waiting for an answer to come to him the way it always did. There was no situation over which he couldn't have complete control and this, surely, was another but no answer materialised in his head. Instead, he just found himself thinking that *he wanted her*. It was something elemental. It defied logic and had caught him on the hop but it was still there, that powerful surge of his body when he looked at her and when he caught her looking at him.

He pushed himself away from the counter top and headed for the sitting room, where she was sitting on one of the sofas with a magazine in her hand and her feet tucked under her.

Although it was not yet completely dark, she had switched on the lights. Outside, with the falling snow, there was a twilight hue that made it feel much later than it was and the scene of roaring log fire and woman curled up on sofa just needed the addition of faithful Labrador to turn it into a picture from a magazine.

She looked up from whatever she was reading and Cesar strolled into the room and sat at the opposite end of the sofa.

'Does it bug you that you can't get in touch with anyone?' she asked, just to break the silence. The way he was looking at her made her stomach flip into knots.

'I'm getting used to it. I might have to start having the occasional retreat without my computer or mobile.'

'But with a change of clothes.'

'That would work,' Cesar drawled. 'I've washed my boxers and I'm more than happy to put them on and stick these things in the wash, but if you find that offensive…' He grimaced at the trousers, which had now seen a night at a club and a stint in the driving snow gathering logs, not to mention the grubby business of chopping them and getting the fire going.

'I'm not sure that that's a very good idea.' Suddenly the room seemed a lot smaller, the fire a lot hotter and her skin as tingly as if electric currents were pulsing underneath it. 'And I haven't got any tracksuit pants that would fit. I…er…'

'So you *would* find it offensive…'

'Not at all. I'm not a prude.' She laughed lightly and reminded herself that he was just a guy and a guy who had been pretty insulting towards her. More to the point, *she* might be able to recognise that obvious sexual appeal of his but her effect on him was rather different. Not only, by his own admission, was she not the sort of woman he found attractive, she was the sort of woman he found the least appealing. He liked them subservient and background. She was independent and outspoken. He had made the most of being cooped up in her house and had seemed to enjoy the unexpected break of having to indulge in doing things which he never did because he could pay someone else to do them for him but that didn't mean that he was no longer the cold-eyed, suspicious man who had quizzed her on her motives. It *would* make him suspicious if she became jittery at the thought of seeing him in a pair of boxer shorts. Which were, in effect, no more revealing than swimming trunks.

'I could always remain safely tucked away in my bedroom until I was fit to come back downstairs,' he murmured, lowering those magnificent eyes of his so that she couldn't tell whether he was joking or not.

Jude made a decision. 'If you give them to me, I'll put a wash on.'

'Only if you're sure…'

'Why shouldn't I be?' She gave another tinkling laugh to indicate surprise that he might think otherwise and stood up, stretching, because her legs were now stiff from her awkward sitting position.

'No reason. I just wouldn't want to embarrass you…' Cesar looked at her with a little half smile and his eyebrows raised, the picture of pious solicitude. 'I won't take them off here. Nothing underneath. Boxers still drying on the radiator upstairs.' His voice was apologetic and polite. 'You may not embarrass easily, but far be it for me to put that to the test. I'll leave them outside the bedroom door. Just give me a couple of minutes...'

He was in high spirits by the time he hit the sitting room, this time wearing the ubiquitous T-shirt and his silk boxers, now dry if a little crisp.

He would never have guessed in a million years that having to play truant from work would have such unexpected benefits. He'd certainly meant it when he'd told her that he would have to start arranging some more down time for himself because he hadn't thought once about any e-mails he might have received, to which he needed to respond, nor had he been particularly bothered by the fact that his cellphone was switched off. He could have contacted his secretary, informed her that she had to get to the office and fill him in on whatever numbers he needed for client contact over the weekend, but he had rejected that idea even before it had fully taken shape. Incommunicado was working just fine for him, as it happened.

He went across to the fire. On the mantelpiece was a selection of books, most of them semi-architectural, a few dedicated to iconic designers and a couple of fictional works. He slotted out one of the architectural ones and was leafing through it when he sensed her by the door.

'You don't mind, do you?' he asked, casually lounging and seemingly engrossed in the print in front of him.

Jude opened her mouth but nothing emerged. Seeing him standing there, with the light from the fire flickering over his hard, bronzed body, made her throat run dry. The tingly feeling was back, this time accompanied by a desperate need to sit down because her legs felt like jelly. She knew that it was absolutely imperative that she stop gaping like a teenager.

It would be mortifying and disastrous if he suddenly looked up and spotted her doing her goldfish impression, right down to the bulging eyes, but she couldn't wrest her eyes away from the fabulous perfection of his body. His stomach was flat and hard, his muscled legs long and lean with perfectly shaped calves and thighs. He stood there, indolently leaning against the wall, and he resembled a classical Greek statue. Living and breathing, she reminded herself shakily.

'No, of course not.' She remained hovering by the door, rooting through her brain for some excuse to vacate the room in favour of some other part of the house, where she could get her breathing stabilized.

'You never told me what sort of design work you do,' Cesar mused, slowly turning to face her. The curtains had been drawn and the overhead lights switched off in favour of the two lamps on the tables either side of the sofa and the standard lamp in the corner of the room.

'You never asked,' Jude stammered.

'Why are you dithering by the door?' He snapped shut the book, tucked it under his arm and strolled to the sofa, where he proceeded to sit down and extend his long legs on the low table in front of him. Then he patted the space next to him, which Jude chose to ignore in favour of the less challenging one on the chair by the fire. Arguing with him, bristling and fending off accusations seemed like a walk in the park compared to the weird, gut-wrenching sensation of having an amicable conversation while looking at his semi-clothed figure.

'There's an architectural theme to your books.'

'I began studying architecture,' Jude said, eyes above waist level, 'but I had to quit because it was too long and I needed to go out to work.' He tilted his head to one side with a show of immense interest. 'My mother had just died and my sister's husband was laid off at just the wrong time because they had a newborn. The proceeds from the house…well, it wasn't much and she needed it a lot more than I did…'

'Tough call,' Cesar said sympathetically.

'These things happen. I really enjoyed interior design so I decided that that was the next best thing and, as it turns out, I'm pretty good at it because I can offer more than just a load of advice about colour and soft furnishings. I can help with all the fundamental stuff to do with restructuring houses so they get my knowledge without the big bill at the end. If a qualified architect gets involved, he usually just has to sign off on drawings that have already been done.' She couldn't resist a smile of pride.

'Talented lady.'

Jude flushed with pleasure at the compliment. 'I get by,' she told him with a little shrug. 'I may not be rolling in money but I've been able to buy this cottage and most of the mortgage has been paid off because my sister's husband went back out to work a year and a half ago and she's managed to repay me the money I gave her. Not that I asked for it.'

'And she lives around here?'

'On the other side of the world, actually. Australia.'

'So you're here on your own…' Was that how she and Fernando had become so close? Two lonely souls gravitating towards one another? He reopened the book, which had been resting on the sofa next to him. 'This place…' he said slowly. 'Where is it? I like it. Like the dimensions of the rooms…' He gave her a lazy look from under his lashes and saw her fractional hesitation before she came across to where he was sitting. Deliberately, he kept the book on his lap, frowning down at the series of black and white photos spread across two pages, so that she either had to circle the sofa and lean over him or else…yes, as she was doing now…sit next to him.

'That's one of my favourite apartment renovations,' she said, keeping her distance, which was awkward because it involved angling her body to see the pictures without toppling onto him. 'Ferrea has managed to combine comfort with modern, clean lines. Some apartments can lack soul if they're too avant-garde but look there…' she pointed to details '…he uses a lot of wood in crucial places and the addition of those beams…brilliant…' She leaned closer to him in her enthusiasm and stiffened as she brushed against his arm. It was just a feathery touch but it resonated through her in deep, disturbing waves which made her pull back sharply.

When she sneaked a look at him, it was to find him staring right back at her with his bitter chocolate eyes. His expression was shuttered and yet, strangely, she seemed able to read intent there and that made her draw in her breath as the colour rose into her face and her eyes widened in acknowledgement of everything that was not being said. Or maybe she was misreading the situation. She had been on her own for a long time. Maybe her imagination had become over-developed in direct proportion to her isolation.

She became aware that she was holding her breath and also that he was still looking at her.

'I guess,' she said, clearing her throat and blinking, 'that's just about one of the few modern places I could actually see…see…er…myself living in…' She gave a nervous laugh and gestured around her. 'I mean…you can tell that I'm the kind of person who goes for the weathered…look…' Her voice faded because he raised his hand and curved it at the nape of her neck. Then he began stroking her, just his thumb against her skin, moving in tiny circles that sent fireworks through her body.

Jude had no idea what was going on but she wasn't fighting

him, and somewhere deep inside she realised that she had been imagining just this moment, when he would reach out and touch her.

She closed her eyes on a sigh as he pulled her gently towards him…

CHAPTER FOUR

For Cesar, this felt *right*. He curled her into him and the kiss, which started softly explorative, became deeper and more urgent. She gasped when they finally broke apart and sucked in a lungful of air.

'What's going on?'

'A kiss. What would you *like* to be going on now?' Cesar questioned softly. It was odd but this was the first time he had ever held a woman with short hair. Had he always been so predictable in his tastes? He glibly criticized his brother for always being attracted to the same type of woman, but he was no different. Neither of them had ever looked outside the box for anything different and he realised that he had never sought anyone who could challenge him. He had never wanted anyone to break through the layer of steel he had concocted around himself. Intimate conversations had been discouraged, as had any games of domestic bliss. Relationships without depth had been safe because they could never threaten the predictable course of his life.

Now this woman.

Cesar frowned, thrown by a surge of complex, conflicting thoughts, but then he relaxed. This felt right because it made sense. He was attracted to her, even though she ticked none of the usual boxes and, more than that, by taking her, wouldn't he be safeguarding his brother from a potential gold-digger? She made all the right noises about not wanting money and said all the right things about just wanting Fernando as a friend, but money was a powerful magnet and, just in case she had the slightest thought of worming her way into Fernando's affections, what better way to prevent that than by making her his own first?

It made no difference to Cesar whether she was after money or not because he, unlike his brother, was well equipped to handle any sort of woman. He, unlike his brother, could handle *anything*.

'We were…talking about designers…' she stammered, reaching out for the first thing she could think of that might restore normality, but she couldn't drag her eyes away from his beautiful face. She felt as though she were drowning.

'So we were…' Cesar agreed. He angled his long body into a more comfortable position on the sofa, never releasing her, just shifting her into position.

With no messy, tumbling hair everywhere, he could really appreciate the grace of her neck, the slimness of her shoulders, the exquisite daintiness of her heart-shaped face.

He slid his hands to span her waist and slowly caressed the satiny smooth skin with his fingers. 'You were telling me about that apartment…how much you admired the guy who designed it…' He gently parted her legs with his thigh, a small but significant movement because now she was straddling him and he could move his leg against her while he continued to look earnestly into her eyes.

Cesar didn't know quite how he was managing to maintain this level of self-control when what he wanted to do was rip off her clothes and indulge in the glory of making love to her.

Nor did he know just how long he had been nurturing those thoughts. When had his suspicions morphed into lust?

The material of her trousers felt abrasive against his naked thigh.

Jude sighed and her eyelids fluttered as the heat and moisture built up inside her until she felt incapable of doing anything but riding the growing tide of desire.

He was moving his leg against her crotch and she liked it. God, how she liked it! She pressed herself against his muscled thigh and a wave of sensuous pleasure drained her of all coherent thought. Her sigh turned into a moan when he placed his hands on her bottom and pushed her down hard against him so that now her swollen, sensitised nub was being massaged even through her clothes.

'Shh...' Jude silenced him, and Cesar looked at her with a mixture of lazy triumph and a powerful, uncontrollable, surging *craving*. Her eyes were closed and she was arched back, the flats of her hands on either side of him so that their bodies only met at that point where his leg was rubbing against her.

Cesar was desperate to touch her but mingled with the conviction that she wanted him was the nagging thought that she really didn't *want* to want him. It was just that her body had managed to ambush her logic. If he began touching her intimately, if he made a move to strip her of that tight little T-shirt that was the ultimate in tease because he could see so much and then the rest was left to the imagination...would she back off? Would her eyes fly open and logic reassert its rightful place?

Never hesitant in bed in his life before, he was taking on board the unaccustomed realisation that he would have to let her come to him. He would have to let her initiate that first move. Whether she knew it or not, she was in the driving seat and he had no choice but to relinquish the steering wheel to her.

The frustration was agonizing, so when she did lower herself, blindly seeking out his mouth, he couldn't resist pulling her against him. His kiss was an assault on her senses as his tongue delved into the softness of her mouth.

Jude groaned. She could feel his hardness pushing against her as she lay down against him and instinctively she reached down with one hand and felt it, then she slipped her hand beneath his boxers and wrapped her fingers around the massive, throbbing shaft of steel.

Her body seemed to be operating on autodrive. Sex with James had been a pleasant business. Nothing like this.

'Don't begin what you can't finish...' Cesar said hoarsely, and Jude opened her eyes and gazed into his.

'What would you do if I decided to walk away?' she teased unsteadily. She had wondered what it would be like to see this big, powerful man in the grip of something beyond his control. She was seeing it now, as she continued to massage him until he was forced to put his hand over hers and squeeze tightly.

'Continue our in-depth...our...'

She scrambled to pull the T-shirt over his head and, for a few seconds, revelled in the sight of him. She ran her hands over his broad chest, loving the hard definition of muscle against bone.

'My turn now, wouldn't you agree?'

Jude smiled and reached to yank off her top, but he was there first, ridding her of it in one fluid movement and stopping her before she could unclasp her bra at the back. Instead, he cupped her breasts and began playing with them, teasing her nipples through the lacy covering.

'Neither of us is going anywhere,' Cesar told her thickly, 'so what's the rush? I want to enjoy every inch of your beautiful body and I want to take my time.' He scooped one small, ripe breast from the bra and almost lost control of himself.

Outside, night was rushing in. In the flickering light, he could see the fine film of perspiration making her face shine like smooth satin. He lowered her breast towards his mouth and felt her tremble under his hands. She was as supple as a cat, her slight, slim body yielding to him as he began suckling on her pink, hardened nipple.

She was hardly aware of him easing her jeans off, although she helped by wriggling free of them and she tried very hard not to be frantic when she tugged down his boxers.

'Maybe we should go upstairs…' she murmured.

'The sofa's more than big enough for the two of us. Besides, why waste a good fire?' He rolled her onto her back and they swapped positions.

Jude looked up with a slow, curling smile as he pinned both her hands above her head and then lowered himself on her so that he could continue to lavish his attention on her breasts.

She kept her hands raised behind her, half hanging off the back of the sofa, even when he had moved his. Arched like this, his mouth on her nipples as he nuzzled and sucked, sent fire shooting through her body.

She couldn't keep still. Little moans escaped as she twisted in a fever of longing and, as he eased himself lower, she curled her fingers into his hair, pushing him down and parting her legs, inviting him to taste her in a way no man had done before.

She shuddered as he trailed his tongue against the flat planes of her stomach, circling it around her belly button. She knew she said something at that point, something that made him give a low, sexy laugh, then his exploring mouth was moving lower until she could stand it no longer and he slipped his tongue into her.

In the same way as she had massaged him with her hand, so he teased her with his tongue, sliding it up and down over the swollen bud until she was bucking against him and gasping with the effort of not reaching her climax against his mouth.

Dimly, she was aware of the fact that there was no contraception to hand. This was a situation for which she had never catered and she wasn't one of those thoroughly modern young women who kept a stash of protective measures *just in case*. There had been no *just in case* episodes in her life before.

She tried to work out whether she was in a safe period and decided that she was, although she realised that her mental arithmetic was a little sketchy just at the moment.

So when he finally levered himself onto her and asked her, unsteadily, whether she was protected, she had no hesitation in nodding.

He thrust into her and began moving deeply and firmly, and then faster as they both surrendered to their bodies. She cried out and jerked up just as he gave one final powerful thrust that sent him over the edge.

He was still breathing unevenly when his shuddering orgasm eventually eased him from its grip, as if he had run a marathon and was struggling to catch his breath.

He turned onto his side and pulled her against him, tucking her leg between his. Her hair was damp against her cheek and she looked drowsy. Drowsy and satisfied, he thought. Ever confident about his abilities in the bedroom, he found himself resisting the temptation to ask her whether it had been good for her, whether it was the best sex she had ever had. Since when had he ever been concerned by crazy notions like that?

'I don't know what happened just then.' Jude could feel her heart beating like a drum inside her chest.

'We made love.'

'I know *that*, but I…I don't *do things like that*. I mean, hop into bed with a man I barely know.' Dawning reality was making her think that she should probably get up and get dressed but he had his arms around her and her body was suddenly lazy and weak.

'Believe it or not, neither do I.'

'You're right. I don't believe it.'

Cesar laughed softly and stroked her hair back. 'Okay, I admit I haven't led a celibate life since Marisol died, but this level of spontaneity…'

'You mean you court your women before you hop in the sack with them.' It was so silent in the cottage that she could almost hear the beating of their hearts. 'Don't you ever get lonely?' she asked, and Cesar stiffened as he felt the push against his self-imposed barriers. This was one of the most intimate questions he had ever been asked.

'You don't have to answer that one,' Jude said quickly. 'Not if you're scared to.'

'Scared?'

'Maybe not *scared*, as such.'

'Of course I don't get lonely! I have a very active life, as it happens.'

'Right.'

'Your tone smacks of disbelief.' But he laughed. He felt too damn relaxed to let her get under his skin. Must be something in the good old-fashioned clean country air that had gone to his head. He stroked her thigh and then pushed her legs apart so that he could cup her between them, just gently resting his hand there. He could already feel himself ready to make love to her all over again, like a sex-starved teenager bedding a woman for the first time.

'Course I believe you. I bet you play lots of sport, go out a lot and have women flocking around at your beck and call.'

'Yes to all three.'

Of course he was just being honest. For a man like Cesar, women were just a pleasant distraction in his life. This sort of situation would be unusual for him and not just because it would have veered wildly away from his normal routine of pursuit and capture, not just because they had fallen together against all odds—it would have been unusual because she wasn't his type.

'Where do you go?' she asked, stifling the discomfort she felt at knowing that she had slept with a man who would walk out of her life the minute the snow stopped falling and he could climb back into that expensive car of his and drive away. 'You said that you go out a lot. Where to? Theatres? The cinema?'

'Theatres, yes. Cinema—can't tell you the last time I went to see a movie. There's not enough time in the day for such mindless luxury.'

In her head she was getting a picture of a man who seldom relaxed and the more glimpses she got of the man, the more she wanted to know more.

'Theatre is a luxury,' she pointed out.

'Theatre is either entertaining clients,' Cesar told her drily, 'or else being entertained by them. Life in the concrete jungle is one great big exercise in back-scratching.'

'Sounds fun.'

'I can think of better things to do.' He grinned and let her know just what he had in mind by reaching out to touch her breast. 'Are you ready for me again?'

'We *could* talk…a bit…'

'Why?'

In that split second, Jude knew that her curiosity had been a mistake. They had made love, done the most intimate things imaginable with one another, but in all other respects they were still worlds apart. Discovering one another was not on Cesar's agenda, at least not beyond the extent of getting to know her in relation to his brother.

'You're right. Why talk when there are so many better things to do? I mean, I've been on my own for a while…'

She stroked his back and felt him stiffen.

'What are you trying to say? Are you telling me that you're using me as a refresher course?'

'What on earth are you talking about?'

Cesar shifted so that he could pull back from her, look her squarely in the eyes. 'You know what I'm saying, Jude. You haven't been with a man for a while and here I am.'

'Ah.' Dawning comprehension. Cesar might find talking a bore, he might use women for recreational purposes only, but he didn't like the idea that for once the shoe might be on the other foot. She knew that it was wrong to encourage him to mis-interpret her behaviour but weren't some lessons in life salutary?

'You *are* quite a hunky specimen…'

'*Hunky? Specimen?…Specimen?*'

'Don't tell me that I'm the first woman to tell you that…' Jude found that she was enjoying the wicked one-off opportunity to have Cesar on the back foot. 'I mean, what girl in her right mind *wouldn't* enjoy a string-free romp in the hay with you? Especially if she happens to find herself marooned with you, so to speak?' To prove her point, she leaned forward and kissed him slowly, lingeringly and provocatively on his mouth.

This was a Jude she didn't recognise. She had taken her relationship with James seriously and one step at a time. She had made sure that she got to know him over a period of time before they progressed onto a physical level. She certainly would never have encouraged him to think that she was using him for sex! Nor would she have hopped into bed with him after a few hours because they happened to be in the same place, at the same time and with the same thing on their minds.

'I don't believe I'm hearing this,' Cesar said repressively but she could feel him responding to that kiss and it gave her a heady feeling of power.

'Why not? *You* enjoy sex with women without any desire or intention of having a *relationship* with them...'

'You're playing with vocabulary.'

'Am I?' Jude gave a perplexed frown. 'Sorry, I thought I was just being honest and straightforward. I always speak my mind. You know that. You said that yourself.'

'I have relationships with women.' Cesar wasn't sure why he was launching into a debate on a non-subject, but he felt self-righteously aggrieved at her spurious accusations. 'Just not relationships that will end up leading down the aisle. You ask any of the women I've dated in the past. They'll all tell you that they had a damn good time with me.' He shot her a wolfish grin that made her blood run hot with desire, but she kept her expression serious. *This* was talking and she knew it was dangerous but she felt driven to get beneath that iron exterior to the real man, even though her head was telling her that it was a pointless exercise.

'If you say so.' She shrugged. 'Talking's overrated anyway,' she told him truthfully. 'You can talk until the cows come home and think that you really understand someone, only to discover that you didn't know them at all.'

'And, on the flip side of the coin, you can spend two minutes in someone's company and realise that you know them completely.' He cupped one of her breasts and teased her pouting nipple with his thumb. The rough abrasiveness of his finger sent feathery sensations all through her body until she could almost feel herself melting.

'Hmm,' she sighed, curling her body against him and moving sinuously against his erection. 'My parents did, you know. One look across that crowded village hall and their future was sealed.'

'Which, theoretically, makes me as good a candidate for everlasting love as your ex. You'd better make sure you don't fall for me.' Cesar realised that he was guilty of making the most provocative statement he could think of but he was still a little irritated when she laughed as if he had cracked the joke of the century.

'Oh, *please*,' Jude said, sobering up but still smiling. 'I would need sectioning under the Mental Health Act if I was ever fool enough to do that.' *Fall for him?* It was a crazy, disturbing thought that made her denial all the more vigorous. 'You're probably the last man on the face of the earth I could ever fall in love with.' Just to silence that little voice in her head that was reminding her that she had managed to climb into bed with him, which would have been unthinkable two days ago.

'I'm crushed,' Cesar murmured, his hand moving down to idly play between her legs. 'You're very bad for the ego. Most men would be insulted to think that they were being used as a stud.'

'But you're not...' And she almost wished he was, but sex for the sake of sex, unsullied by any annoying emotional complications, was the kind of language he understood.

'I'll come back to you on that one...'

This time round their love-making was fierce and urgent. When he had touched and caressed every inch of her body, he rolled her so that she was on top of him, driving down on him while she continued to kiss his face, his neck, the broad span of his shoulders.

He didn't know what time it was when he eventually surfaced. His legs felt stiff and he had to angle himself off the sofa because she had fallen asleep on his shoulder. As he moved, she stretched and made a soft sound, then squirmed back into sleep mode.

For a few seconds Cesar stood, naked, looking down at her, trying to get her measure.

She bristled and hissed like a wildcat, but then there had been moments when she had been shy and cautious and tentative. One minute she acted the stammering girl, the next she was telling him that he was nothing more than a pick-me-up for someone who needed a little sex. Who the hell was she?

One thing for sure—if she had decided to seduce Fernando, for whatever reasons, the poor boy wouldn't have stood a chance. As he watched her, she stirred and opened her eyes. There was no post-coital smile on her face, nor was she making the slightest effort to entice him back between the sheets.

This in itself was a little annoying. Cesar was accustomed to women using all manner of guile to keep him in bed once they had managed to get him there in the first place.

'Have you checked the weather?' They had been lying on the throw which she used as an attractive cover for the squashy sofa and she half wrapped it round herself now and wriggled into a sitting position.

She could, shamefully, have stayed lying there on the sofa with him for the rest of the day but she had felt when he had eased himself off and had kept her eyes closed, feigning sleep.

She wasn't sure how she had managed so spectacularly to jump into a pot of boiling water, but jump she had. They had made love and as they had dozed, entwined like the perfect happy couple, she had had time to think and they *weren't* the perfect happy couple. In fact, they were neither perfect nor were they a couple in any way imaginable. Even the happiness part was debatable because, while she had been on cloud nine when they had been making love, reality had had time to do its job and yank her very firmly back down to earth.

Cesar was a highly sexed man and, caught up in an unusual situation, he had taken what he had sensed had been on offer. Somehow he had managed to twig that she was attracted to him and he had acted on that nebulous feeling with the unerring instinct of a man accustomed to women falling over themselves to get near him. No phone, no computer—what better way to pass the time than making love? He was a man who would be able to distance the act from emotion, but what about *her*?

She had wanted him and had made love to him because he fascinated her. There were feelings wrapped up in the melting pot and she knew that she had to stand back and take stock before those inconvenient feelings dragged her down deeper.

'About to.' He walked across to the window and squinted at a black and white landscape. 'Snow's stopped.' He dropped the curtain and turned to look at her, pink and rumpled and cool as a cucumber.

'That's good. Look…' Jude licked her lips nervously '…about what happened…'

'You mean the business of your using me to satisfy your sexual needs…?'

'It wasn't quite like that,' Jude admitted grudgingly.

Cesar strolled to where their heap of frantically discarded clothes were piled together on the floor and extracted his boxers, which he slipped on. 'Well, that's some much needed balm for my battered ego,' he said, fishing through the bundle and separating them.

'We both got carried away. Cooped up here, with the snow outside…a bit like people who do crazy things when they're on holiday. It was just something that we'll have to pretend never happened.' She took a deep breath.

'And what if I don't feel like going along with the pretence?'

'Why wouldn't you?' She had fed her curiosity and was beginning to see how women could be brainwashed by men who just weren't good for them. She intended to get her speech in before he could deliver his.

'What if I think that what happened between us was pretty good? What if I think that there's no conceivable reason why we have to *pretend* it away?' He shrugged. 'So the snow stops and life gets back into gear…' He strolled towards her. 'Are you telling me that that would make a scrap of difference to the chemistry between us? In fact,' he continued smoothly, 'are you telling me that if I decide to kiss you right now, you're going to turn away because you've been able to tell yourself that you are no longer attracted to me?'

Jude hadn't bargained for anything but ready agreement from him and she looked at him in some confusion.

'That's not the point.'

'Then what is…?'

'The point *is*…' Now he was perched on the sofa next to her, his weight depressing it so that her body inevitably slid against his. 'The point *is*,' she repeated patiently, 'we both acted out of character. I don't…I'm not the kind of girl who just hops into bed with someone on the spur of the moment and yes, I know I might have given you the impression that I was just using you, but I don't do stuff like that. The fact is that if I choose to get involved with a man, then I want more out of it than just a romp in the hay.'

'Clarify.'

'We're different people, Cesar. We don't think along the same lines and what you look for in women is not what I look for in men.'

'Oh, well, everything's as clear as mud now.'

'Don't pretend you don't know what I'm saying. You distract yourself with women…'

'Because I'm really deeply unhappy and lonely…haven't we been here before?'

Jude could feel all her well thought out arguments begin to unravel at his mildly amused, mildly indulgent tone of voice. This was not the aggressive reaction she had expected and now she felt as if she were on thin ice. Wasn't that huge ego of his supposed to respond with predictable fury?

'You're right on one count,' Cesar said thoughtfully. 'Leaving aside the loneliness, deep unhappiness issue, I don't get involved with women because I don't want anything long-term out of the relationship, but do you…?'

'Do I what?'

'Want something long-term out of this?'

'I'm not going to waste my time with someone who's a commitment-phobe and, like I said, you're not the sort of man I'd envisage being a life partner,' Jude told him bluntly. 'I don't mind admitting that I've made a mistake and move on from there.'

'Move on to…what?'

'To someone I think I can build a relationship with, and if it doesn't come to anything, then that's fair enough, just so long as we both start with the same intentions. No one knows what the future holds but we can all start out with high hopes that it's going to be leading somewhere. You don't, Cesar. You start out with the assumption that all your relationships are destined for the bin and they do. You've been married and it was wonderful and since nothing will ever compare to that, then as far as you're concerned, there's no point in trying. You take what you want and then you walk away, and please don't tell me about all the lucky women who have thoroughly enjoyed being with you and would never have dreamt of asking for more.'

A dull flush had spread across Cesar's high cheekbones. 'Finished?' he asked coldly.

'You probably think I'm being stupid…'

'Your choice what decisions you make with your life but while you're in the mood for sermon preaching you might want to think that, while you're waiting for your dream to come true, life's passing you by.'

'You're right. My decision.'

'I was about to go and have a shower. After that, I'm going to go and see how deep my car's buried under the snow.' He had never begged for any woman in his life before and Cesar wasn't about to start now. She had made her point perfectly clear. 'Just out of interest, what *is* your ideal guy?'

'Someone kind and thoughtful,' Jude said defensively. She wasn't sure how he had managed it, but it no longer felt noble to be holding out for the perfect man. Was she wasting her life waiting for a dream? And if Cesar was that far off the scale in terms of suitability, then how was it that he had the ability to make her heart beat faster and her pulses quicken? How could he make her feel so *alive* when all her common sense pointed to the fact that he was all *wrong*?

She was beginning to feel faint as she took stock. She might say one thing and tell herself that she believed it, but somehow the man had crawled under her skin. What had started out as dislike had turned into something else and now she was very much afraid that she had committed the fatal sin of beginning to fall for him.

'Someone who doesn't think that he's God's gift to womankind,' she carried on fiercely. 'A gentle kind of guy...' Except James was like that and where had *that* ended? Cesar was nothing like that and yet...

'Why did you sleep with me?'

'You should go have your shower.'

'I will just as soon as you say it.'

'Okay! I slept with you because you're...you happen to turn me on! Satisfied?'

'Perfectly. You forget, I only know how to use women. I just wanted you to say it aloud, though, so you can remind yourself that sometimes having fun is its own reward. An empty bed is never grateful for the moral high ground.'

He headed for his shower. He damn well needed something to cool him down! He had managed to get the last word, but it had been an empty victory.

Of course, he told himself, rubbing himself dry with the towel and then glaring at his reflection in the mirror, women like that were bad news for a man like him and he should have been thanking her for being honest and upfront. And, hell, who was he to complain about jettisoning someone because they didn't fit the bill? He had jettisoned countless numbers of women in the past, maybe not with quite such unadorned frankness, but it all counted for the same thing.

Stuck inside this cottage had made him stir crazy! The minute he got back to civilisation, he would forget the woman, climb back onto the dating bandwagon, from which he had been away for a disturbingly long time, rediscover the guy who worked hard and played hard and didn't get involved with long, futile discussions about emotions, which frankly were best left alone.

Hell, he hadn't even been able to shave for nearly two days! His facial growth was now more than just designer stubble. He was beginning to look and act like a caveman.

With any luck, the snow would disappear as quickly as it had come and he would be able to leave this God-forsaken part of the world and resume his life.

At least, he thought, bringing all his will power to bear to eradicate her annoying, lingering image from his head, one thing was sure. She wasn't after his brother in search of elevating her lifestyle. Whatever nuances he had sensed between them had been in his imagination. The only thing the woman was after was a knight in shining armour. She wasn't into the finer art of subtlety. Oh, no. If she had been in any way, shape or form interested in his brother, then Fernando would have been married and en route to papahood by now!

He decided that he would let this whole business be a salutary lesson to him—keep close to the devil you knew…the ones you didn't were too much of an infernal headache!

CHAPTER FIVE

JUDE later wondered how she'd managed to get through the remainder of their snowbound isolation, but two weeks later, chewing it over in her head as she had been doing ever since she'd watched him close that front door quietly behind him, she knew that he had been the one to pull it off.

He had disappeared for his shower and, when he had returned, he had followed her heated plea to the very last letter. She had asked him to pretend that nothing had happened and he had. He had checked on his car, which had taken a long time because of the banked-up snow. In his absence, she had tidied the little sitting room and each cushion she had plumped had been one more gesture towards putting away for good the wild moments they had shared together. In under an hour, the room had been restored to its original impersonal cosiness, with the absence of the wretched throw, which she had put in the wash.

She had even lit two scented candles because she could detect the aroma of their love-making, and she wanted no reminders.

They had eaten in the kitchen, discussed the weather in civilised voices and retired to their separate bedrooms at the earliest possible hour.

And every ultra-polite question he had asked, his fabulous

eyes shuttered and expressionless, had been like a knife twisting inside her. At the time she had wondered how on earth he could have been so utterly detached, but now, thinking about it, she knew why. Cesar wasn't the sort of man who was swept away on great tides of emotion. Nor had he invested any feelings in her. He had slept with her and had enjoyed it, and he probably would have carried on an affair of sorts for a while after, but that hadn't been enough for her and he had accepted that with a casual shrug of his shoulders because he could take her or leave her. He was a man for whom emotional involvement was an unnecessary complication. He had been down that road and, whether he would ever admit it or not, had buried his ability to *feel* with his wife.

Overnight the snow had begun to melt and in the morning she had awoken to find him fully dressed and ready to leave. He had already been out to try the car and had managed to get it pointing in the right direction. He had left the engine running, he said. Her interpretation of that was that the faster he could get away, the better. A running engine was the equivalent of a taxi outside blowing its horn.

Since then she had heard nothing from him, although she had been to visit Freddy and Imogen and it seemed that the fate of the precious trust fund was assured. Cesar hadn't fallen over himself in admiration of the bar, but nor had he demolished the idea after five seconds, which had been Freddy's fear.

She was busying herself with her latest project, half thinking about her drawings and half thinking about Cesar, when the phone rang. As usual, there was a heart-stopping second when she thought that it might be *him*, even though she had told herself that he couldn't possibly call her because he didn't know her number, so common sense told her that of course it wouldn't be him.

But nor had she expected a distraught Freddy stumbling over his words until she asked him to slow down because she couldn't understand a word he was saying.

'I am at the hospital,' he said shakily.

'Hospital? Why? What's wrong? Are you hurt?' Jude felt a rush of panic as in the space of seconds she contemplated the worst. She swivelled her chair around and leaned forward, clutching the receiver to her ear.

'It's Imogen. She's been rushed in.'

'But the baby's not due for another couple of months.' She felt a fine film of perspiration gathering on her forehead.

'You have to come, Jude,' Freddy told her with rising panic in his voice. 'She's in theatre right now and I'm going out of my mind with worry!'

'On my way.'

'And you have to…to tell Cesar…'

'Tell him *what*?' Just the mention of his name made her nerves flutter. When she had last seen Freddy, he had told her that while Cesar had reluctantly given his blessing to the bar, he hadn't wanted to press his luck by telling him about Imogen because who knew what eruptions might follow. Cesar, in over-protective mode with the family fortune, was an unpredictable animal. It was, he had told her, a tactical omission and not an outright lie. So now, with dismay, she had some inkling of the favour that was about to be asked.

'I'm in no frame of mind to explain about Imogen,' he said and Jude could hear the worry in his voice. Placid, good-natured, girlie Imogen was the quiet but steady rock in their relationship. Freddy, with his effervescence, had never been a candidate for winning any awards when it came to holding out in a crisis. Her heart went out to him as she imagined his panic.

'I know I probably should have confessed everything the

last time I saw Cesar. He was being particularly receptive but...but...'

'Okay. And I'll get to the hospital as soon as I can. You'll have to give me your brother's number, Freddy...'

Fifteen minutes later and Jude was on her way to the hospital. She hadn't bothered to change out of her dungarees, just slinging on a wooly jumper over them and wrapping a long trailing scarf around her neck. The snow had completely disappeared and after the cold snap had come a spell of unseasonably warm weather. Everywhere people were tut-tutting about global warming and complaining that they never knew what to wear when they went out.

She had yet to phone Cesar. That was something she had decided to defer until she got to the hospital and at least made sure that Freddy and Imogen were going to be all right. Both her cellphone and the scrap of paper on which she had written Cesar's various numbers were burning a hole in her pocket, hovering on the edge of her anxiety, just enough to make her feel queasy.

She made it to the hospital in record time but naturally took ages to park. By the time she ran through the doors of the maternity ward, she was totally stressed out and a pressure headache was beginning to build in her temples.

Freddy found her before she found him and he looked as frightful as she'd figured he would. The baby was fine, he told her, but had been rushed off to intensive care. It was a girl.

His eyes filled up and he looked away quickly. 'I've been told to have her christened immediately...just in case...'

'Don't do the *just in case* scenario, Freddy,' she said quietly, giving him a hug and then standing back with her hands on his arms. 'You'll just make yourself even more worried. How's Imogen doing?'

'She's lost a lot of blood…'

'But she's…going to be okay, right?'

'They won't say. The next few hours are important. Jude, I have to get back to her… Have you…?'

'I'll phone him in a minute. I wanted to get here first and make sure that both of you were all right. All *three* of you,' she amended with a reassuring smile. 'Is Imogen awake? Will you give her my love? I'm going to stay here for a while, Freddy…' She hoped that didn't sound grim but he seemed relieved by that and left her a few minutes later with the unenviable task of calling his brother.

Jude made her way to the café, her nerves stretched to breaking-point. The smell of the hospital made her feel faint. In a room upstairs her closest friend was hanging on and in another room the baby she and Freddy had looked forward to having was struggling with the complications of being born prematurely. Nowhere in a hospital was it possible to feel calm. Even in the cafeteria there was the ominous feeling of people waiting for news, good or bad.

She bought herself some coffee and retreated to the farthest corner table, out of earshot, not that anyone would be likely to pay her conversation the slightest bit of attention.

Freddy had given her a handful of numbers, but in fact the first number she dialled—his mobile number—was answered within a couple of rings.

Down the line, the reception so clear that he could have been sitting next to her, came that rich, low, velvety voice that had reduced her to jelly. She hadn't thought, especially with everything going on and her head in a whirl, that it would have the same effect now, but it did.

'Cesar, it's me. Jude,' she clarified, just in case he had forgotten her existence.

Miles away, in his London office and with his secretary sitting opposite him, Cesar felt himself freeze. He gestured to his secretary to vacate the room and she did, closing the door behind her.

To his intense frustration, the past two weeks had been hellish. His formidably controlled mind had refused to obey orders and the memory of her had seeped in through all sorts of cracks and crevices which he hadn't known existed. He had found himself losing concentration during meetings, an unheard of occurrence, and at the least convenient moments his imagination would steal in like a silent thief to capture his thoughts and he would have to physically rouse himself away from the temptation to gaze out of his window and just think. Of her. The smell of her and the feel of her, which lingered in his head like a fever he couldn't shake.

Now, hearing her voice on the line, brought all his rage at his weakness rushing to the surface.

'And to what do I owe the honour?' he asked coldly.

'Look, I know you're probably surprised to hear from me…'

'How did you get my number?'

'That's not important. Cesar, something's happened…'

He detected the urgency in her voice and he restlessly sprang to his feet and walked across to the impressive floor-to-ceiling windows of his plush office, which overlooked the hustle and bustle of the financial district. Somewhere inside him a knife twisted.

'What are you talking about?' he demanded, his breathing uneven. 'Where the hell are you?'

'I'm…I'm at the hospital…' There was no point explaining anything down a telephone. The minute Freddy had asked her to call his brother, Jude had realised that she would have no option but to see him again, even if seeing him was the last thing she wanted to do. 'Would you…would you be able to get here? I'll explain everything when I see you. I'm sorry if I caught you on the hop…'

'Name.'

'Sorry?'

'The name of the hospital. What is it?'

He scribbled it down on a piece of paper and shoved the paper into his pocket. He had several meetings lined up for later in the afternoon and was scheduled to leave the country later that evening. None of it mattered.

'Tell me what this is about,' he said in an attempt to regain his self-control. 'I am a busy man.'

'I know and I'm sorry but I'd rather not say on the telephone, Cesar. But it's important.'

'I'll be there in half an hour.'

That brought a reluctant smile to Jude's lips. 'How are you intending to do that? Fly?' She had an image of him swooping through the clouds like Superman. He might be able to do most things but that one was definitely out of his reach.

'Correct.' Cesar was already calculating how long it would take to get there on his private helicopter. Not long. 'Where will I meet you?'

Jude was about to ask him what he meant when it clicked that he would probably own a fleet of helicopters and private jets. He was, as he had said, a busy man and busy men didn't waste time dealing with the vagaries of public transport if they could possibly avoid it. 'I'll be in the cafeteria,' was all she said and, with all the necessary information imparted, she was treated to the abrupt silence of disconnection. He had asked relatively few questions and had given no indication of curiosity, for which she was thankful. Of course, he must suspect that Freddy was involved and, whilst she felt for him having to make a journey with maybe some pretty dark thoughts in his mind, she also knew that what she had to say would, at least, be more bearable than what he possibly suspected.

Only when she was on her second cup of coffee, which was surprisingly good and surprisingly cheap, and after she had once more visited the ward for an update, of which there was none, did she begin to feel the pounding of nerves.

She aimed for distraction by reading one of the tabloids provided on a table by the cash tills, but she couldn't resist the temptation to glance up every five seconds, it seemed, and search the doors to the cafeteria for him.

She told herself that this was a meeting of necessity and that if Cesar threw a fit because his brother had chosen to keep Imogen's existence quiet, then she would be the one in the firing line. Didn't they say that the messenger was always the one to be shot?

As luck would have it, she had finally been distracted by the gossip page when she became aware of Cesar's presence by the shadow thrown over the table. She looked up slowly, giving herself time to fix her expression and harness her composure, but it didn't work because the very minute their eyes met, she felt all her self-control give way to a sickening attack of nerves.

She had hoped that in the interim her lively imagination had exaggerated his powerful, brooding beauty and the ferocious impact it had on her nervous system. It hadn't. If anything, in his dark tailored trousers and crisp white shirt, with his jacket hooked carelessly over one shoulder, he looked even more dangerous and magnificent. And utterly cold.

She half rose and then sat back down with a tight smile. Hell, he had been so *civilised* the last time they had been in the same space together that the very least she could do would be to return the favour with a little sangfroid of her own.

'Would you like some coffee?' she blurted out, only belatedly realising that it was a pathetic attempt at a greeting since she was neither a waitress nor a hostess.

'What I *want*,' Cesar grated, 'is to be told why I am here.'

He pulled out the uncomfortable plastic chair and sat down. He had spent the entire trip in a state of heightened anxiety and was ridiculously relieved to see her looking fit and well, if haggard. There were shadows under her eyes and her short hair was tousled, as though she had been running her fingers through it. His eyes skimmed over her outfit, which appeared to be some kind of workman's overalls.

'It's a long story, Cesar…'

'Is my brother all right? Just answer me that.'

'Freddy's…fine.'

'And…*you*…?' He felt himself struggle with the question.

'I'm fine, thanks for asking.'

'Then what the hell is going on?'

Jude tried hard not to react to the imperious tone of his voice. Of course he was going to demand an explanation! Cesar being Cesar, he wouldn't ask polite questions or tiptoe around with pleasantries!

'I'm going to tell you! If you'd just stop *snarling*.'

'I don't have the time or the inclination to sit here while you try and get your thoughts in order.'

'It's…it's about your brother, Cesar.'

'You said that he was fine.' For some reason, he had assumed that there was nothing wrong with his brother, had assumed that, because she had made the call, then whatever the situation, it concerned *her*. Now, with the muted sounds of people shuffling in the cafeteria and the depressing smell of antiseptic cleaners mixed in with unappetising food, Cesar contemplated the possibility that his ferocious anxiety had been misplaced.

In a split second it dawned on him that there had been many opportunities in the past to try and heal the distance between Fernando and himself but that maybe his time had run out for second chances. He clung to the fact that she had told him that his brother was fine, even though they were sitting in a hospital so clearly he wasn't quite as *fine* as she said.

'He is. Sort of.'

'Fine. Sort of. *Get to the point, Jude!*'

'It's not that easy!' And particularly so when he was glaring at her as if she had mutated into something unsavoury that had crawled out from beneath a rock. She guessed that he had had no choice but to be polite to her when he had been holed up under her roof, but now he had options and he had chosen the option of showing his full-blown aggression. She had dragged him away from his precious work, was blathering and dithering instead of telling him why she had done so and he wasn't about to exert any patience with her because time was money and she had cut into his time.

But how on earth was she supposed to explain about Imogen in a few brief sentences? She had vaguely thought about what she was going to say. Now she wished that she had jotted it all down on some paper so that she could just hand it to him to have a read and then ask questions. A bit like a comprehension exam.

'Do you remember asking me…why Freddy seemed so keen on sorting out the matter of his trust fund as quickly as possible? When he had always been happy to go with the flow and let you settle all his bills?'

'Go on.' This wasn't what he had been expecting by way of an explanation, but then he might have guessed that anything to do with her would defy all his laws of predictability.

'Well, there was a reason.' She looked at him warily. It was hard to believe that for a window in time she had felt relaxed enough to share anything with him. Right now she was looking at a stranger, a cold, distant, watchful stranger. 'And I can understand why Freddy did…well, what he did…'

Cesar, reading between the lines, seeing the uncomfortable expression on her face and the anxious fidgeting of her hands, adding it to the fact that he was currently sitting on an orange plastic chair in a hospital, came to the only conclusion his logical mind could find.

'Are you trying to tell me that my brother has had some sort of money problem that he's kept to himself? I knew he gambled, but has it got out of hand?' Cesar cursed softly to himself. He had controlled his brother's lifestyle for his own good, making sure that he kept an eagle eye on his outgoings so that he could forestall any potential problems. But what if his brother had *had* financial problems? What if there had been a shortfall somewhere and he had been too scared to come running to him, knowing what his reaction would be? That would make sense. In a moment of rare self-examination, Cesar acknowledged that he could be unsympathetic and dismissive.

'Has he got into some kind of trouble and ended up in hospital because of it?'

'Freddy hasn't gambled for months, Cesar. No…'

'Drugs, then. Is that it? Is that why I'm sitting here?' He raked his fingers through his hair and for a moment she felt a powerful tug on her heartstrings as she looked at this big, controlled man torn by incomprehension and deserted by his usual self-assurance.

She reached out and touched his hand. For a second there was a bond between them, as if a bridge had sprung up between the massive chasm that was dividing them, then he shook off her hand.

'Stop, Cesar,' Jude said firmly. She sat on her hands just in case they decided to do something crazy again without her permission. 'You're jumping to all sorts of conclusions. Freddy hasn't got a gambling problem and he isn't a drug addict either. The opposite, in fact. He's as focused as he's probably ever been in his whole life and that's the thing... there's a reason why he's changed...'

'Just spit it out, Jude, because I'm getting tired of the endless riddles.'

'He's in love.'

'*He's in love?* And he's in hospital because of a...what... *broken heart*? Tell me, who exactly is the object of my brother's affections?' His eyes narrowed suspiciously on her face and Jude looked back at him, outraged at the implied insult in that questioning gaze.

'Not me, if that's what you're thinking, Cesar! Do you imagine that I would have...could have....if...' She took a few deep breaths and told herself that she shouldn't be offended because Cesar was just being Cesar. Suspicious to the point of absurdity.

'He's in love and has been for a long time with a girl called Imogen.'

'That's impossible,' Cesar dismissed, pushing back his chair so that he could extend his long legs at an angle. 'The name means nothing to me.'

'Don't be so superior, Cesar!' Jude snapped. 'You live in a bubble, do you know that? A magical world where you think you know everything there is to know about everybody!'

Far from having any impact on him, Cesar lounged back in the chair and shot her a look that questioned whether she had taken leave of her senses. On several counts, he felt considerably relieved. Firstly, his brother was fine. Secondly,

Jude was fine. Thirdly, for a second there that whole *Fernando in love* thing had done something crazy to his composure, for a second there he had thought that Jude was the woman involved. She wasn't.

'I'm really struggling to see where all this is going. So my brother fancies himself in love. He's been there before and he'll go there again.'

'He hasn't and he won't and you still haven't asked why you're sitting here if the only reason I wanted to see you was to tell you that Freddy's found the girl of his dreams.'

Cesar had the grace to flush. Relief seemed to have distracted him from the main issue. In fact, relief on several fronts had weirdly distracted him from what should really be annoying him, namely the fact that, at great personal inconvenience, he had sequestered the company helicopter on a mission that could probably have waited.

'You said. Her name's Imogen.'

'And she was rushed to hospital today to deliver their baby, which was born prematurely.'

The silence that greeted this slice of information was deafening. For once, Cesar was utterly and completely dumbstruck and Jude didn't know whether to laugh at his expression or duck for cover.

'You're kidding.'

'Do I look as if I'm kidding? Freddy called me up this morning in a complete state of meltdown. He's been here for the past few hours, out of his mind with worry. Hence he volunteered me to tell you…to tell you the truth about Imogen…'

'Why was I kept in the dark about this?'

'Could you *keep it down*, Cesar?' she hissed. 'Have you forgotten where we are?'

'Is there somewhere else we could go?' he asked abruptly.

'No, there isn't. At least not within walking distance and I want to stay here. Imogen is my closest friend. You once asked me how I met your brother. Well, it was through Imogen and the reason this was kept from you was because Freddy was afraid that…'

'You both lied to me.'

'We didn't *lie*…' Jude didn't want to get into this offshoot of what she had to say. She had known, almost within minutes of meeting Cesar, that any form of deception would not have sat easily with him and, whilst she had chosen to label it, as Freddy had, *a slight evasion*—a slight *temporary* evasion— she was uneasily aware that she had been an accomplice to something Cesar might well consider insupportable.

'I think I need to go and see my brother.'

'It's not a good time to start an argument about this. In fact, I won't allow it.'

'You won't allow it?'

She recognised this as a tone of voice that could have halted an army in its tracks. However, Jude wasn't about to let Cesar loose on Freddy. Even if he gave her his word that nothing would be said about the revelations, she knew that, inevitably, he would be physically incapable of *not* expressing an opinion. Cesar lived in, and was accustomed to living in, a world in which he had absolute freedom to say what he wanted. Today, she determined, wasn't going to be one of those days.

'That's right. I'm not going to let you confront Freddy…'

'You misunderstand me. I never said anything about confronting my brother…'

'You don't have to,' she said bluntly. 'Freddy's not in a very good place right now and he doesn't need you making things worse.'

Cesar was lost for words. Never in all his adult life had anyone forbidden him from doing anything. The words *allow* and *Cesar* had never actually occurred in the same sentence and here she was now, glaring at him like a headteacher dealing with a recalcitrant pupil.

'I think we should talk,' Jude continued, ignoring his outraged expression. 'I can explain why Freddy chose not to disclose any of this to you…'

'As did you. Even when we were in your house, making love.'

Jude went red. She didn't need any reminder of that. Her mind did a very good job on its own of not letting her forget.

'Maybe it *would* be a good idea to find somewhere else to talk,' she conceded, half to herself. 'We're occupying seats other people might need more than us.' And, besides, she wanted privacy to speak with him, even though she knew that no one was listening or would care what they were talking about, even if they were sitting right next to them at the same table.

'Scared I might blow a fuse?'

'I know you wouldn't do that.' At least, not at that very moment in time. She stood up. 'I'll just go and see Freddy, let him know that I won't be around for an hour or so and I'll meet you back here.'

Cesar knew that there was nothing to prevent him from going with her but he contented himself with a curt nod. He needed time to himself to think, at any rate. On the surface was the business of being deceived, but scratching the surface was the far more overwhelming reality that Fernando had a baby, that he had managed to keep secret an entire chunk of his life because…

He watched her get eaten up by all the people coming and going and rubbed his eyes wearily with his fingers.

It was turning out to be one hell of a day. Rather than churn over in his head all the thoughts which seemed too big for him to absorb, he flipped open his cellphone and put a call through to his secretary, whom he had left wearing a baffled expression and holding a dossier of paperwork which, she had stammered, was urgent. Efficient as she was in every way possible, the one thing she apparently couldn't deal with was a boss acting out of character.

Her bewilderment was almost audible down the line when he told her that all his appointments were to be cancelled until he informed her otherwise. Anything important should be e-mailed to him. She couldn't have sounded more shocked if he had told her that he was about to take a trip to the moon.

He snapped shut the phone just as Jude was weaving her way back towards him.

For the briefest of moments, just the span of the blink of an eye, he forgot everything. He only saw *her*, her slight figure which, as he knew from first-hand experience, was as sexy as hell, the stubborn, elfin attractiveness of her face, at present lost in distraction, the short hair that could have looked disastrous and instead was inexplicably appealing.

What the hell was she wearing? He'd never seen such a shapeless garment in his life before, not helped by the oversized jumper she had thrown on over it. A jumper which he recognised as one of those hanging on a hook by her front door.

She focused on him at the same time as he reined in his mutinous train of thought. How the hell could he be distracted at a time like this, when there were a thousand and one questions bouncing around in his head?

'I've spoken to Freddy,' Jude said, not sitting down. She grinned. 'Things are looking good for both mother and daughter. Their baby's going to be kept in hospital for at least a couple of weeks, maybe longer, but the doctors say she's doing incredibly well and Imogen's smiling, which is always a good sign. I've told Freddy that we're just going to grab a coffee somewhere in town but that we shouldn't be long.'

She didn't add that Freddy had wanted to talk to his brother himself because she wanted to make absolutely sure that she had had a chance to put Cesar in the picture and hopefully deflate any tendency to erupt. If Cesar knew that Freddy was no longer in quite the same state of shock, she was pretty sure that he wouldn't now be getting to his feet and putting on his jacket.

'My car's in the car park.' She turned away and killed the treacherous thought that maybe, just maybe, there was a little part of her that *wanted* to carry on talking to Cesar, even though she had no idea how relaxing the conversation was going to be. To be brutally honest, even though she knew that the conversation was probably going to be hellish. Just being in his presence, like an addict driven to feed an unhealthy habit, was irresistible.

'I never asked,' she said as they headed towards her car, 'how did you manage to get here so quickly?'

'Helicopter.'

'I'm sorry to have dragged you away from your...meetings...'

'I know. You already apologised. Is *that* your car?'

Ah, something on which to focus that was neither the delicate situation at hand, which she would leave until they were sitting in front of their energy-boosting coffees, nor her rapidly beating heart which was signalling to her, with every sickening thud, that she was still as knocked out by the man as she ever had been.

She could lose herself in a pointless but much needed quibble about the incredulous scorn in his voice.

'Have you got a problem with that?' She faced him squarely, hands on her hips, before unlocking the door the old-fashioned way, as central locking was still a dream when her Land Rover had hit the roads. As were most other automobile gadgets the rest of the Western world took for granted.

'Lots of problems,' he said, defusing the situation, much to her annoyance, 'but that definitely isn't one of them.'

CHAPTER SIX

WITHIN half an hour they had parked and were making their way to a coffee shop. The short drive had been conducted largely in silence. Cesar seemed heavily preoccupied with his thoughts, staring through the window, and Jude was content to skip the stilted conversation about nothing in particular.

'They haven't decided on a name for the baby,' she said eventually, to break the silence. 'Freddy thinks maybe Maria after your mother and Florence after Imogen's mum.'

'What is she like, this woman…?'

'We can talk about that…once we're sitting down, having a coffee.'

'I need something stronger than a coffee!'

Jude nodded. Well, it *was* nearly five-thirty. She veered away from the coffee shop and towards a restaurant/bar which opened all day for food and drink. It was spacious, very modern, comfortable and, at this hour, virtually empty. By seven-thirty it would be packed solid with an after-work crew.

'Right,' Cesar said as soon as the waiter had scuttled off to get their drinks—mineral water for her and a whisky for him. 'You were going to tell me what this woman is like. I presume not the sort you would bring home to meet the parents if

Fernando has kept her a secret.' He shot her a twisted, cynical smile. 'No one keeps a woman locked away unless they're ashamed of her.'

'It's nothing like that. Of course Freddy's not ashamed of Imogen! Why would he be? She's a wonderful girl and I should know that better than most. I grew up with her.' The bottle of mineral water looked dangerously insufficient to cope with Cesar on full throttle.

'How ironic to be singing the praises of someone who, until today, didn't exist as far as I was aware. Suddenly she's out of the cupboard and you're telling me that she's the next best thing since sliced bread. Now, why would that be?'

'Because of the trust fund.'

'Ah. So you and my brother connived to keep this all under wraps until the trust fund business was settled, is that it?'

'We didn't *connive*, Cesar.'

'No? Well, I'm racking my brains to think of a more appropriate word.'

'You're not going to make this any easier for me, are you?'

'Did you expect me to?'

'No,' Jude admitted. She picked up her glass and swirled it around for a while, watching the bubbles scatter on the surface, then she took a sip of the water. 'And that's why Freddy felt that he couldn't confide in you.'

'I have never tried to run my brother's love life.' Cesar shrugged magnanimously. 'He has always been free to do whatever he wants to do with any woman he wants to.'

'Just so long as whatever relationship he had remained transitory. He told me that his role was to marry a woman of independent means.'

Cesar's mouth thinned. Yet more confidences, more whispered secrets. 'I never laid down any rules about that.'

'But it was understood. Cesar, there's no use pretending that you're not really protective about all that money in your bank account! You practically accused *me* of being a gold-digger the first time we met!' She told herself to calm down and not get off the topic because she could hardly hold the torch for being transparent when she had kept Imogen's importance to Freddy to herself. 'Imogen doesn't come from the sort of privileged background that you would have found acceptable. At least, that's what Freddy thought.'

'He should have told me so himself, man to man. He wanted the trust fund—no, wrong use of word here—*needed* the trust fund, presumably because the woman in question was up the spout, but instead of laying his cards on the table, he chose to approach it through a side door. In cahoots with you.'

Jude reddened uncomfortably. 'It wasn't like that. He knew that you wouldn't approve. In fact, he knew that you'd probably try to intervene and of course you had the trump card because you pulled all the financial strings.'

'Forget about whether the woman came from a privileged background or not. There must be some other reason why he never breathed a word of her existence to me.' They could keep going round and round in circles about the upside and downside of enormous wealth, about the measures taken to protect it, but they would get nowhere because, in the end, they would have to differ. Reality meant no time for useless discussions. Cesar needed to flush out the whole story and then decide how he played it from here.

He was, he acknowledged, shaken to the core and, much as he felt concern, as any human being would, for a woman who had been through what must have been a nightmarish ordeal, he still had to think with his head.

Naturally, the woman sitting opposite him wouldn't understand that. Anyone who'd spent her life looking for a knight in shining armour clearly had no use for her head.

'He thought that you would write her off as being after his money because of…of the way she looks…'

Cesar sat back and finished his whisky in one long swallow. Now they were getting somewhere. 'And how would that be?' he drawled. 'No, let me guess. Blonde hair? Big blue eyes? Lush, sexy body?'

'Something like that,' Jude mumbled. She took a deep breath and said in a rush, 'And she worked in a nightclub. Actually, that was where they met.' What was the point of a partial truth?

'In a nightclub. Doing what? With her blonde hair and blue eyes and sexy body? Hmm. The books, maybe? Or a receptionist?'

'Not quite.' She looked at him, at his shrewd, cold, calculating, fabulous eyes and mentally winced. 'She…um…waited on tables, so to speak.'

'So to speak…?'

'Well, if you must know, she was a stripper. Of sorts. Nothing crude, of course.'

'No. Far be it from me to think anything of the sort.' A picture was beginning to form in his head and he didn't like it. He had no problem with Fernando dating a stripper—hell, he was a red-blooded male and had always had a taste for blondes—but what had been the stripper's motives? How long before she *forgot* to take her contraceptive pill and *accidentally* fell pregnant?

'I can see what you're thinking, Cesar, and you're wrong. They're head over heels in love and Imogen is one of the nicest people you're ever likely to meet. I grew up with her and there isn't a mean, avaricious bone in her body!'

'Except that now she's had a baby and presumably was behind Fernando's sudden urge to get his hands on his trust fund?'

'That was *his* idea. He'd been thinking about doing something for himself…'

'And naturally coming to work for the family business was never one of the plans mooted…'

'You know how Freddy feels about office work. The thought of sitting behind a desk like you do, staring at a computer screen and going to meetings…well, it was never going to be his cup of tea.'

Cesar had to stop himself from giving her a description of exactly what he did. Instead, he focused on the problem at hand.

'Anyway, he was going to tell you everything…'

'I'm sure. Just as soon as I gave him the green light to get his hands on his money. Have you any idea how much he will be worth?'

'Lots?'

'And, of course, by the process of association, how much this friend of yours will be worth.'

'Her name is Imogen.'

Cesar shrugged. 'Does he intend to put a ring on her finger?'

'Of course he does!'

'Dammit! The boy should have come to me before he got himself embroiled in this situation!'

'He's not *embroiled* in anything!' Jude snapped indignantly. 'He's walked into this relationship with his eyes wide open and he's *happy*. Doesn't that mean anything to you? No, it probably doesn't,' she said acidly. 'I guess you've forgotten what it was like to be head over heels in love and looking forward to starting a life together.'

'Marisol was embraced by the family,' Cesar said. 'There

was no question mark over her head as to whether she had inveigled her way in because she could smell the whiff of bank notes.' He thought, with some surprise and discomfort, that whereas she had always been at the back of his mind, the rosy picture against which every woman he had ever dated was measured, this had not recently been the case. Recently, his head had been filled with the image of another woman, one who didn't fit the mould and, he told himself with remorseless iciness, fitted it even less now. A woman capable of sleeping with him and holding her secrets to herself. Her extremely *costly* secrets.

'And you're very fortunate that you found the perfect love match. Did you think that you'd be able to dictate to Freddy whom he should marry? What background she should have? What the colour of her hair should be?'

'Don't be ridiculous.'

'I'm not being ridiculous! This is exactly what he was afraid of.'

'That I would have his welfare at heart?'

'That you wouldn't give him a chance! He's not a kid any more, Cesar! And you liked his jazz club idea. Freddy told me that you did. It's well thought through and he's put a lot of effort into costing it. Do you think a *kid* would have been able to do that? He's even gone into detail about what sort of acts he would have and he'll make a success of it because his heart's there, and he has so many of the right connections.'

'Where are you going with this?'

'Give him the benefit of the doubt.' Jude knew why she was fighting their corner. They weren't there to do it themselves. Imogen was closer than family to her, and while it might well have been better for Freddy to have spoken to his brother *man to man*, as Cesar had put it, his priority at the moment had to be the woman he loved and their tiny baby daughter. But she still had her own problems to deal with, her own tortured thoughts to put to rest, her own screwed-up heart to try and piece together. Just sitting opposite him was sending her nervous system into frantic overdrive.

'Have you *ever* treated him like an *adult*, Cesar? Capable of making the right decisions for himself?'

Cesar flushed darkly and scowled at her. 'I'm beginning to see why he sent you to do his dirty work. You're like a pit bull.'

'That's a horrible thing to say!' Jude looked away quickly, her eyes filling up. Where was a handkerchief when you needed one? Or even a bit of wretched self-control?

She wiped her eyes harshly with the sleeve of her jumper and then stared down into her half-empty glass of water. She only saw the pristine white handkerchief when it was thrust in front of her and, when she stubbornly refused to take it, she only realised why he had withdrawn it when she felt his fingers on her chin, tilting her face up so that he could carefully dry her eyes.

The breath caught in the back of her throat. His eyes were the colour of dark, bitter chocolate and she felt as though she might drown in them given half a chance.

'I apologise for that last remark,' he said gruffly. 'It was uncalled for.' She wasn't a crier. Cesar didn't know how he knew that but he *just did*. She might have crazy girlish notions of love and romance but that didn't make her soppy, which was why the tears still glistening in her eyes had had such an effect on him.

And God, now that he was touching her, he wanted to touch more. He wanted to dip his head and capture her mouth with his, feel the coolness of her lips and the sweetness of her tongue against his. He wanted to slip his hand behind those hideous overall things until he felt the warmth of her breast and then he wanted to touch that ripe pink nipple, stroke it with his fingers until it hardened and made itself ready for his mouth.

He had to make a Herculean effort to drag himself back down to earth.

'You can keep the handkerchief.'

Jude gathered her scattered wits and tried to think straight even though she could still feel where his fingers had been in contact with her skin, leaving their mark as boldly as if she had been branded.

'Okay.' Cesar sat back and looked at her carefully. For a second there, he had been caught up in some rip tide of sensation but he had to remember that he wasn't born yesterday, whatever sob story he got fed. 'I admit the jazz club idea might work out if Fernando is prepared to go the distance and do the work and I'm willing to give him credit for trying to get some sort of focus in his life, but I still have serious misgivings about this woman...'

'You won't when you meet her,' Jude told him quickly, sensing the smallest of chinks in his armour and determined to exploit it before it disappeared. 'Which, hopefully, will be soon.' Her worry over Imogen and the baby was playing havoc with her emotions and she felt another weeping jag approaching. She diverted it by blowing her nose and standing up. 'In fact, we should get back to the hospital, see what's going on. Freddy hasn't called so I'm hoping that everything is going to be all right.'

In fact, it was another hour before they did, finally, get to see Freddy. The traffic back to the hospital was a nightmare and the car park was an endless line of cars trawling in search of an elusive space.

Jude looked at Freddy's face and knew immediately that

Imogen was through the worst. She also knew, without having to be told, that he wasn't looking forward to having the in-evitable chat with Cesar, but she had done enough to smooth the path and after popping in to give an exhausted Imogen an enormous hug and then stopping in to see the very, very tiny baby with masses of dark hair, which made her want to cry all over again, she headed back to her cottage.

She didn't know what was being said between the two brothers. Cesar was as hard as granite and with little time for the grey areas that made up most people's lives. His own life was so ordered and so controlled that he expected everyone else's to be the same and was intolerant of any deviation.

So why did she…feel so acutely tuned in every time she was around him? Because he was intransigent and autocratic? Because there was a lump of ice where his heart should have been? Because she was in love with him?

The realisation was not accompanied by the clap of thunder or an explosion of fireworks. It just sneaked into her head quietly and unobtrusively, confirming what she had known in her heart for a while. He filled up every part of her and she couldn't talk herself out of it or reason it away.

He represented just the sort of person who, on paper, was the last man on the face of the earth she should have been at-tracted to, but whoever said that love was contained and logical like a game of chess?

Seeing him that afternoon, she had felt as though her world had been tilted on its axis. Now, back in her house, she wondered miserably if it could ever be levered back into position. Even when she had been gritting her teeth and trying not to explode at his all-knowing, all-consuming *pigheadedness*, she had still felt something inside her melting and taking flight.

And when he had touched her…

She sternly reminded himself that the reason he had touched her in the first place, accidental contact though it had been, was because he *had made her cry*. She had been emotional, anyway, having to deal with everything that had taken place, and being *insulted* had just been the final straw. He had called her a *pit bull*! She masochistically replayed the insult over and over in her head in the hope that she might shore up her weakened defences but she was having little success as she made herself something to eat, when she heard the rap of her front door knocker.

Her immediate thought was that it would have to be Freddy.

Sandwich forgotten, she wiped her hands on the dungarees, which she had yet to get out of, and flew to the door.

She blinked in confusion at the sight of Cesar standing on her doorstep. For a few brief seconds she almost wondered whether her mind was playing tricks on her, but that didn't last long.

'I thought you'd want to know what's been happening at the hospital.'

'Sure.'

'Then why don't you invite me in?'

'How did you get here?'

'I borrowed Fernando's car. He's going to be spending the night there.'

She felt her heart begin to pound and contemplated telling him that he had caught her at a bad moment, that she was on her way out, but *where*? And still dressed in her *dungarees*? And wouldn't the lie be more of an indication of how much he affected her than if she treated him in much the same manner as she would treat anyone?

'How is Imogen? The baby? Has there been any improvement? Would you like something to drink? Tea? Coffee?' She could *feel* him behind her as she walked back to the kitchen, avoiding the sitting room, which would be too much of a reality check for her.

'Imogen is steadily improving. The baby is doing as well as can be expected. Better. Apparently, she is a healthy birth weight for…a baby of that prematurity. I'll have a coffee.'

With her back to him, aware of him pulling out one of the chairs and sitting down, Jude said tentatively, 'And how was Freddy?'

'How was he about…what? His girlfriend? His *child*? Or his cover-up?'

Jude stiffened, but she didn't swing round to face him. Instead, she continued making them some coffee, only slowly turning around when she could hand him his mug.

'I thought that maybe you had come here to tell me that you had had a change of heart, had listened to some of what I had to say. If I'd known that you were just going to repeat the same things you said to me earlier on…'

'I listened to what you said,' Cesar told her flatly.

'And?'

'I naturally expressed my disappointment that he hadn't seen fit to tell me about…this bit of his personal life…' He held up one hand to stop her before she could speak. 'Don't worry. I'm not the monster you think I am. I appreciate that my brother is going through a difficult time at the moment. I was…very controlled…'

He looked exhausted.

'Naturally I mentioned that I would have to think carefully about releasing the entire trust fund at his disposal…'

'Oh, great. In other words, you got your message across loud and clear that you don't trust the woman he loves and wants to marry.'

'In other words, I let it be known that I'm willing to sink

money into this venture of his—certainly he will get a proportion of his trust fund…'

'And Imogen? Did you get to meet her at all?'

'I thought it better to leave her to recover first.'

'And you're going to head back to London now? Or are you
going to stick around for a few days, moral support for Freddy?'

Cesar hesitated. His sparse retelling of the facts had not
allowed for the unexpected empathy he had felt towards his
brother nor for the truth, which was that he had paid her words
a great deal more attention than she probably assumed. A
month ago, he would have dealt with his brother according to
the facts as written on a sheet of paper. Namely a blonde
stripper, an unknown quantity, had got herself pregnant and,
to that effect, his brother wanted to get hold of a vast sum of
money in the naive belief that he could throw it at some ill-
conceived venture, half of which could feasibly end up in the
hands of a woman who had taken advantage of his gullible
nature. Ergo, no trust fund.

But something in him seemed to have shifted.

When, for instance, had his brother started fearing him?
How had they reached the point where a fundamental life
change could be kept hidden?

Cesar had heard the condemnation in Jude's voice and it
had got his back up. It had also given him pause for thought.

Yes, he had been incredibly lenient with Fernando. Indeed,
for the first time in many years, they had embraced on parting.
And, before he'd left the hospital, he had actually gone to see
the baby at the centre of all the fuss and had stood watching
it for an inordinately long time in the incubator, amazed that
something so small could be so perfectly formed.

Of course, he would reserve judgement until he had met
the mother of the child, but he now found himself in the

position of being prepared to give the woman both his brother and Jude held in such high regard the benefit of the doubt.

All in all, and hot on the heels of cancelling all his appointments until further notice, his secretary would have been reaching to call the medics were she to see him now.

But underneath it all, and against his better judgement, he could still feel a thread of anger running through him like poison that Jude had deceived him.

He conveniently sidelined the thought that he had justified sleeping with her—*seducing her*—because he had believed that he might extract whatever she was hiding. The only thing that occupied his mind now was the fact that she had lain in his arms, had made love to him and still managed to conceal something potentially highly damaging to the Caretti empire. She would doubtless call it loyalty to his brother. His experience with the money-grabbing women that circled him like hawks had taught Cesar to call Jude's secret-keeping a deliberate act of treachery.

And rumbling beneath this was his anger that she had turned him down, had swept aside their love-making as if it had been an unfortunate disease, something passing that needed to be eradicated by pretending it had never taken place.

'I might just stick around…' he drawled, looking at her coldly. 'After all, I'm going to have to make my own value judgements on this person.'

'I told you…'

'I know what you *told* me but surprisingly I'm finding it hard to believe a word you have to say.'

'That's not fair!'

'No? You haven't got an honest bone in your body, have you, Jude?'

'I explained to you why I did…what I did.'

Cesar knew that this was a conversation destined to go nowhere. He also knew that he *was* being unfair, at least to her. And he didn't quite understand why he couldn't leave it alone. He shouldn't have made the trip out here. There was nothing to gain from a pointless confrontation—but he had got into his brother's car and it had been as though his rational thought processes had closed down.

'Look at the big picture from *my* point of view,' he suggested in a voice that would freeze the fires of hell. 'You and this woman have been friends since childhood.' He drained his coffee and stood up, aware that he was on a roll and that he should make an effort to stop. But, looking at her... It enraged him that he could still *want* her, after all of this. He had never felt so out of control in his life and it wasn't a good feeling. He didn't understand it and he didn't need it. The woman had cast some sort of spell over him and he wanted her conclusively out of his life.

He began walking towards the front door. He knew that she would follow him and she did.

'You tell me that I should take your word for it that the woman is as pure as the driven snow, innocent of any ulterior motives.' He turned to look at her and leaned indolently against the door frame. She had that ferocious look on her face—an expression that suggested that, given half a chance, she would have grabbed the largest, heaviest object to hand and slugged him with it. 'The fact that she met my brother in a nightclub where she works for a living taking her clothes off...'

'She doesn't *take her clothes off*! At least, not *all* of them...'

'Immaterial. You get the gist.'

'I think you should leave.'

'And I will. When I'm finished saying what I have to say.'

'I might have guessed that you didn't come here just to

bring me glad tidings,' Jude said bitterly. 'I might have guessed that it would have just been too much to have sympathised with Freddy and just be happy for him.' Had she actually been fool enough to have imagined that he had wiped her eyes *with tenderness*?

'Don't get me wrong. I would be overjoyed if I thought that Fernando was about to embark on a life of undiluted joy and fulfilment with a woman who loved him for the person he was and not the significant amount of money he brings to the equation. And believe me when I tell you that I'm really going to be totally impartial when it comes to sizing up the situation…'

'As impartial as any dictator is ever likely to be…' Jude muttered under her breath, forcing Cesar to lean towards her words. Which he didn't but somehow he could guess its tone.

'But I can't help wondering whether a conspiracy of sorts was involved…'

'*A conspiracy of sorts?* What on *earth* are you talking about?'

'How am I to know that you two didn't contrive a convenient meeting with Fernando? You would have known his name and, even if you didn't know his pedigree, it wouldn't have been hard to guess that he had money. My brother in a nightclub is an open book. I should know. I've had the unhappy pleasure of being with him in one once. A few minutes on the Internet and you could have sourced his background in under ten seconds.'

'I can't believe you're telling me this, Cesar!' But she could. At least, she could believe it of the man standing in front of her like an implacable rock, his face harshly condemnatory.

'Why?' he demanded in a silky voice. 'Why can't you believe it?'

'Because you should *know* that I'm not that type of person! We've been through this.'

'So we have, but think about it—how much do I *really* know about you? How much do I really *know you*?'

Jude felt cut to the quick by that remark. Did he mean it? Surely, after all they had shared, he knew that she would be incapable of such a horror? Her back stiffened as she adopted a defensive pose. No, she was *not*, absolutely not, going to justify herself to him! But the thought of seeing him walk away with the worst things in his mind made her want to weep.

'If you really think that about me, Cesar, then what can I say?'

It wasn't what he wanted to hear. The truth was, he didn't know *what* he wanted to hear.

'So true. What *can* you say?'

'You put so much importance on money, Cesar. You can't understand that, at the end of the day, it doesn't really mean very much. Yes, it can get you the company helicopter and the designer car, but those aren't things of any value.'

'Still going for the altruistic line, Jude? I might have believed you once, but in the light of what's unfolded, you'll have to excuse a certain amount of cynicism on my part.'

'Why? Why do I have to excuse it? You think the worst of me. You think that I would do anything for a bit of money.'

'Everyone has their price.'

'That's a horrible thing to say.'

'Is it? And here I was thinking that I was being utterly realistic.' He looked down at the glowering face and smiled grimly. 'What a shame.'

'What is?'

'Shame that you don't agree with me, because if everybody has a price then you would discover that I could be a very generous lover...and we made such good lovers, didn't we, Jude?'

He reached out and touched her face.

Jude froze. For a while, all she felt was the perfection of his skin against hers, reminding her that she had given her soul to the devil. She wanted to curve into his touch, hold his hand and lead him to her bed.

She pulled away sharply, her breathing uneven and painful, and placed her hand firmly on the door knob. She couldn't actually open the door as he was still leaning against it, but he stepped aside and she pulled it open quickly, shaking.

'How long do you plan on staying?' she asked tightly.

'Why? Would you want to take evasive measures?'

'Can you blame me?'

'Maybe not.' Cesar shrugged. He had said what he wanted to say. More. Too much. And some of it had left a sour taste in his mouth.

'Just...' she looked up at him, her eyes clear and steady despite the fact that her thoughts were all over the place '...don't let whatever you think about me affect your decision about Freddy's trust fund. Or your opinion of Imogen.'

'Still fighting the fight?'

'Still hoping that there's a place inside you that I can appeal to, some bit of you that isn't totally jaded.'

Cesar flushed darkly. He didn't like the picture she had conjured up but, in all fairness, he could hardly blame her. However, that was not something he intended to impart, so he gave her a curt nod and left through the open door, straight to his brother's car.

From the doorway, she watched as the car revved and then swung neatly round, doing the fastest three-point manoeuvre she had ever seen in her life. When she closed the door, she felt drained. The day had started badly with Freddy's call and it had gone downhill since, picking up speed with Cesar's appearance on the scene.

Now, she was shattered. The nagging headache which she had managed to keep at bay was returning with a vengeance. She needed and wanted nothing so much as to have a hot bath and climb into her bed, but then what would she do once there? Stare up at the ceiling in the darkness and think about him? Think about what he had said? He surely couldn't have meant it…could he? Could he really think that she had plotted and connived with Imogen to cheat someone out of his money?

He would meet Imogen and realise that he had been wrong, and in fact some small part of her sensed that everything he had said had been an overreaction to the bombshell that had been laid at his door.

He had lashed out but he had lashed out at *her* and that really hurt because, even if she never saw him again, and it was unlikely that would happen, he had been left with the wrong impression.

Which made her think of all those long days lying ahead, days in which he would play no part, a life in which he would have no say.

He had been cruel and blinkered and cold and she tried very hard to resurrect some good, healthy dislike but she couldn't. She couldn't resurrect anything but the way he had made her feel when his fingers had touched her skin.

CHAPTER SEVEN

WITHIN a fortnight, both Imogen and the baby were out of the hospital. Little Maria was already beginning to gain weight and Freddy, the proud father, was fast-tracking his jazz club venture, which had now received Cesar's financial backing thanks to the release of a fair amount of the trust fund.

'I'm on probation,' Freddy had told Jude sheepishly, 'and I can't say I blame him. After all, I *have* spent a goodish amount of my adult life squandering my money, so he's going to be careful, really.'

Whatever Jude's personal feelings about Cesar, she was very happy for Freddy. Maybe Cesar had found himself cornered but, whatever the reason, he had cut his brother some slack and, better than that, had been thrown into the novel situation of having to defer to Freddy on his expertise when it came to the practicalities of opening a club. It was doing Freddy's sense of self-worth a power of good.

And today was the Big Day. A little sooner than expected, and a lot smaller than Freddy's extended family might have wanted, but still happening. A register office affair in Marylebone, followed by a lavish lunch at one of the top restaurants, which had closed its doors to the public for the day.

The honeymoon, Imogen had told her, was to be put on hold for a few months but, radiant with her newborn, she didn't seem to mind in the slightest. Nor did she seem in the least bit critical of her brother-in-law-to-be. He was, she had told Jude, very charming and she couldn't understand why there had been all this fuss about him in the first place.

Jude had refrained from pointing out that, yes, sharks might not bare their teeth *all the time* but that didn't mean that they weren't capable of inflicting grievous bodily harm. She should know.

It was all now one Big Happy Family. Winners all round. Except, of course, for *her*.

She gazed at her reflection in the mirror. She looked like someone recovering from a bad bout of flu. Hollow eyes, face a little too thin, anxious expression.

In a little under two hours she would be standing in that register office, and it would be the first time in nearly three weeks since she had seen Cesar, although the passing of time had done little to soften the blow of his final departure from her life. Every cruel word he had said had been imprinted on her mind with such force that she relived the moment even in her sleep.

She had chosen her outfit carefully. It was a loose jade-green woollen dress, just reaching her knees, and with an attractive empire line that gave it a youthful appearance. A sensible buy, all things considered. She had even bought herself a fancy coat, something in which she would never have thought to invest, but she felt that she might need courage when it came to meeting Cesar and what better to give courage than an image-boosting outfit?

Now all she had to do was apply sufficient make-up to deal with the worried face.

By the time her taxi arrived she looked a great deal better than she felt. The dress lived up to the expectations she had had when she had bought it two days previously, as did the high black shoes and the fancy coat. Her black bag was a little too oversized to be labelled anything other than useful, but what was she to do? She still had her hundred and one things to stuff in.

The worst of it all, she thought, was that she *had* to meet Cesar. She couldn't go along and hope to get lost in the crowd. She *had* to meet him and, for the sake of her sanity, she *had* to talk to him.

She looked at that little, perfectly innocuous piece of plastic on her dressing table and felt the same shiver of fear as she had when she had bought it two days ago.

It had not occurred to her at any point that she might be pregnant. She still wasn't too sure when the notion had begun to form in her head that her period was overdue. Even then, she had uneasily put that down to stress. Wasn't that supposed to affect the body in mysterious ways?

In fact, she was still telling herself that she had absolutely nothing to worry about when those dark blue lines informed her that, yes, she had something to worry about. A great deal to worry about.

Since then she had done nothing but oblige. She had worried.

She had also replayed Cesar's last conversation with her, in which he had accused her of conspiring with Imogen to con Freddy out of his money, some hideous joint venture, which she was certain Cesar couldn't possibly believe.

She told herself repeatedly that he had overreacted because he had been enraged by what he had seen as a case of deliberate deception, that people often said things in the heat of the moment which they didn't mean. Not really.

But it was down to *capability*, wasn't it? He might not really believe that she had conspired to do anything with anyone. In fact, he might have zoomed off in his car, come to his senses and realised that the idea was ridiculous, but at the back of her mind she wondered feverishly whether he thought that she was *capable* of manipulating someone else for her own personal gain.

If he thought that, then how was he going to react when she broke the news to him that she was pregnant?

She had told him, when they had made love, that she was protected. She hadn't exactly explained that she had believed herself protected thanks to the ancient and apparently wholly unreliable method known as *the rhythm method*. He had probably assumed that she was on the contraceptive pill, although why he would assume that she didn't have a clue, considering she had told him just how long it had been since she had slept with anyone. But assume it he must have or else he would have taken charge of contraception himself.

Cesar wasn't looking for commitment, let alone an unwanted pregnancy. In fact, when it came to women, Cesar wasn't looking for anything beyond sex.

The ride to the register office was a nightmare. There was an awful lot of traffic, giving her ample time to stare vacantly out of the window and turn over in her mind the various hideous scenarios that could be awaiting her.

She almost wished that she had made an appointment to see him in his office although, at the time, she had wondered whether he would have even taken her call.

She had opted for today because she had known that he would be there and would have to see her, have to talk to her. Somewhere quiet after the reception was over. At any rate, it didn't make a difference *where* the conversation happened, she told herself now as her stomach churned away. There was no suitable place.

The guest list had been narrowed down to twenty-five people. Some relatives from Spain, close family, and then friends. A trip was planned for later in the year to visit the rest of the family, when Maria was a little older and more able to handle the change of environment.

When the taxi eventually pulled up outside the building, Jude could already see the guests congregated on the steps. At the top of the steps was Cesar, talking to Imogen, one hand in his pocket, his coat lifted by the breeze.

Jude got out of the taxi and took a deep breath before walking the gauntlet from the pavement to the entrance, noticing that, while Cesar briefly broke off his conversation to glance in her direction, he very quickly returned to what he was saying to Imogen, making it clear that while he had noted her presence, he was indifferent to it.

So time, she thought wretchedly, hadn't diminished his bitterness towards her.

He had made his peace with his brother, accepted Imogen as his soon-to-be sister-in-law, and yet the olive branch was visibly not being waved in *her* direction.

She was the last to arrive and offered her apologies to Imogen, while smiling down at a bundled-up little Maria, who was beginning to fret, waving her fists around, her tiny face puckered into a cross frown.

'I've only just fed her,' Imogen confided, 'but she's already hungry again. She eats like…well, like Freddy…' Imogen laughed. 'Are you okay? You look a little drawn, Jude.' This in hushed whispers as they headed indoors, out of the bright but cold sun.

'Just working really hard,' Jude said in a strained voice.

Her eyes darted towards Cesar's back. 'You know how it is...' She hadn't breathed a word of what had happened between herself and Cesar, and Imogen, thankfully, had been too busy to ask questions.

'We'll have to go out soon,' Imogen promised. 'When my life gets a bit less frantic. I feel pretty strong now, but it's amazing how a little thing of just six and a half pounds can turn an adult into a zombie.'

'Well, you look very glamorous for a zombie,' Jude said truthfully, smiling. Radiant, in fact.

And for the next forty-five minutes or so she was spared the agony of dwelling on her situation. The service was short but heartfelt and the couple looked deliriously happy. In fact, even an ingrained cynic like Cesar would have been hard-pressed to think that they were anything but truly in love.

Jude wasn't going to put that to the test, though, by meeting his eyes. Indeed, she kept hers well averted from his dark, striking face, although, as she signed the registry book, she was all too aware of him standing next to her like a block of implacable, unforgiving granite.

She wasn't entirely sure when she would draw him to one side and, like a coward, she kept her distance for as long as she could and as much as was physically possible, given that they were both seated opposite one another at the same table.

She wittered away with seemingly endless enthusiasm to one of their cousins, a nineteen-year-old boy who was heavily into football, something about which she knew precious little but was learning fast by asking all the right questions and displaying all the right interest.

Every so often her eyes would slide of their own accord to Cesar's dark, unbearably handsome face as he engaged the people around him.

She could barely appreciate the wonderful meal, which seemed to stretch on for eternity, course after course after course, and then the toast, a short, witty few words given by Cesar in which no reference was made to Imogen's far from illustrious background or the suspicions that had driven him to assume the worst of their relationship. The man was a consummate actor, Jude thought acidly, charming the crowd in the same way that he had charmed her out from behind that wall which she had erected around her emotions and behind which she wished she was still firmly secure. His own wall was obviously made of far sterner stuff.

It was nearly five by the time the meal was cleared away, at which point her stomach was doing a very merry jig.

She had barely uttered a word to Cesar but, as he glanced at his watch, a sure prelude for him leaving, she followed him to the restaurant door and tentatively placed her hand on his arm.

In the process of slipping on his coat, he turned to her and looked from her face to her offending hand and then back to her face.

'Cesar...hi...' She licked her lips nervously, traipsing along behind him as he left the restaurant. 'How are you?'

'As you can see, never better. Is there something you wanted?'

'You're not still angry with me, are you?'

'Why would I still be angry with you?' Dark, hard eyes clashed with hers. 'You over-estimate your importance, Jude.' Naturally he had known that he would be seeing her but it was still a bad moment for Cesar. She looked more fragile than he remembered, which made him think of her vulnerability when she had lain in his arms. It was a thought he did not want to entertain and he slashed it before it could take root by recalling her deception. He had been taken in by that honest, transparent face and her blazing outspokenness. Never let it be said that he wasn't a man who didn't learn from his mistakes.

He felt duly fortified by that thought and stared down at her icily.

'I…Cesar…we need to…to talk…'

'Do we?' He looked at his watch, just as he had in the restaurant, reminding her that he was probably off to do something. It was Saturday evening and she didn't imagine that he would be spending it alone. In fact, that was something Jude had studiously avoided thinking about. Another woman in his arms was just too much to bear.

'I know you've probably got something to do…somewhere to go…' She invited disclosure.

'Nothing and nowhere that you need know about.' He signalled to his driver, who magically appeared as if out of thin air. In fact, Cesar was looking forward to a meal on his own at an Italian restaurant close to where he lived and an evening in front of his computer, downloading e-mails and reading three reports. This despite the fact that he had been invited to several company affairs which, he knew, might have improved his ongoing foul mood but which had seemed impossibly tedious. Too tedious to attend.

'Of course. I was just being polite.'

'Well, consider yourself relieved of that particular burden.' His driver hurried around to the passenger door and pulled it open for him but, instead of getting into the back seat, he found himself leaning against the car door and looking down at her. 'As far as I'm aware we've covered pretty much everything there is to say, wouldn't you agree?'

'Not *everything*, as a matter of fact.'

'No?' In a minute his car would be moved on. Traffic wardens were very hot in this part of London. Still, he found he continued to loiter, watching her derisively although he had told himself, at irritatingly frequent intervals over the past couple of weeks, that he was well rid of her.

'Maybe we could go and grab a…a coffee somewhere…' Jude offered, even though she had already had two cups after the meal and knew for the baby's sake she really couldn't have any more caffeine.

'I'm trying to think of a single reason why I would want to have a coffee with you.'

Jude rested her hand on the open door. 'Because I want to talk to you and it's the very least you owe me.'

Cesar gave an incredulous laugh. 'Run that by me again?'

'You might just want to shove me out of your mind, but we…we're going to keep meeting up every so often and we need to try and work out how we can do that without ignoring one another. If we ignore one another, Freddy and Imogen are going to start asking questions.' It was the only thing she could think of to say because she wasn't about to drop her bombshell on a busy road in central London with his driver waiting impatiently inside the car.

'You'd better get in,' Cesar said impatiently. 'In a minute we're going to cause a traffic jam.'

She ducked down past him into the back seat of the Bentley and shuffled over so that he could sit next to her. It was hard to tell whether he had decided to talk to her because what she had said made sense or whether he had just got fed up of standing outside his car, obliged to speak to her because clever positioning of her hand prevented him from getting into the car and slamming the door in her face.

'I…I gather you and Freddy have reconciled your differences…' Jude began hesitantly.

It seemed pitiful to be indulging in small talk when there

was something far more important to discuss, but she wasn't going to just blurt it out. If she could somehow get him to thaw just a little bit towards her, it would, she reckoned, make things a lot easier.

'I was given precious little choice.' Cesar leaned towards his chauffeur and instructed him to go to the restaurant, then he turned to look at her. 'Presented with a fait accompli, I could either have stuck to my guns and deprived Fernando of his chance to prove himself or else release his trust fund and give him the independence he wanted.' He shrugged elegantly. 'If he were man enough to get a woman pregnant, and I gather that it was not entirely an unplanned event, then he will have to be man enough to handle his finances and raise a family.'

Everything was very civilised, but Cesar's eyes remained cold and shuttered.

'And…what about Imogen? Have you softened your opinion towards her?'

'Is that why you wanted to talk to me? So that we could compare notes?'

Jude looked away, but it was difficult. His closeness, the intimacy of being in the back seat of the car with him, those deep, black, penetrating eyes—it affected her like a drug seeping into her veins and making her thoughts woolly.

'I thought you would have been a lot less forgiving than you were.'

Cesar was loath to admit it, even to himself, but so had he. In all events, he had seen his brother distraught with worry at the hospital and then afterwards had seen them together, the way they looked at one another, and had grudgingly admitted to himself that maybe some things weren't as black and white as he cared to think.

Furthermore, even in her weakened state, Imogen had

managed to get him on his own and had suggested—no, *insisted*—that she sign a pre-nuptial agreement. She had also, to his surprise, on some paper, worked out a pretty accurate formula for what she thought his brother should be given from the trust fund and it roughly coincided with his own estimate. He had had to do a quick rethink on his preconceived ideas.

'I will, naturally, be taking an active interest in my brother's venture,' was all he said, 'at least until it's up and running.'

'Freddy says that you don't know a huge amount about how clubs are run…' she said with a little smile.

Cesar felt himself grudgingly descend from his polar iciness and he admitted drily, 'It's true. Fernando has discovered the one area of expertise in which I am fairly ignorant and he's naturally revelling in the discovery. In fact, I think it's made his day.'

'Who can blame him? Living in your shadow must have been a tall order.'

'I'll take that as a compliment.' He knew that this was how she had managed to get under his skin. Cesar, in his daily life, was surrounded by people who bowed and scraped and put themselves out to be included in the magic circle that surrounded him. Jude, albeit unwittingly, seemed to carry a metaphorical pin around with her, specifically designed to burst his rarefied balloon.

'It is,' Jude agreed readily. 'I never thought I'd hear you say that you were ignorant about anything, so that means that there must be even more dimensions to you than I thought.'

'*Even more?*'

The car pulled smoothly up in front of a small bistro, sparing Jude the embarrassment of having to explain her backhanded compliment.

After that brief respite her nerves were beginning to kick

in again, but she forced herself to remain calm as they went in. Cesar was obviously a regular and they were treated to the best table in the restaurant, a small one tucked away at the back where the noise level was lower and two oversized potted plants gave the illusion of semi-privacy.

'I can't eat a thing,' she said.

'Can't you? I didn't notice you stuffing yourself at the reception.'

He'd noticed how much she had eaten?

'I'll just have some…some orange juice, I think.' She snapped shut the menu and then stared down at it, as if in search of inspiration.

'So…' Order for some calamari and drinks placed, Cesar sat back in his chair, one arm loosely draped over the back, and looked at her. 'Are we succeeding in this important mission of acting like civilised adults?'

'Did you really mean it when you said that you thought I'd been involved in some sort of plot with Imogen to fleece your brother of his trust fund?'

'Is that why you wanted to talk to me, Jude? Because you wanted to clear your name?'

'Amongst other things,' she mumbled.

'Amongst *what* other things?'

'Why don't you answer my question?'

Cesar looked at her carefully. Hell, it was no skin off his nose if he told her the truth. Anyway, like it or not, she had a point. She and his brother's wife were close friends and he envisaged that his relationship with his brother was set to improve. They were certainly going to be thrown into each other's company more than they ever had been before, with this whole jazz club situation. Chances were high that he and Jude would bump into one another now and again. The baby's christening, for a start, would be a big family occasion. It made sense to drop the hostilities.

And it had clearly been preying on her mind. That instantly made Cesar feel pretty good.

'I confess I may have said one or two things that possibly weren't entirely accurate, that being one of them.'

'What were the others?'

'Has this been worrying you?' he asked casually. The calamari arrived, just the right amount considering he had eaten a hefty lunch only a few hours previously.

He imagined her losing sleep over what he had said, tossing and turning at night, unable to function by day and desperate for him to release her from her misery. His mood went up a couple of notches. It made a pleasant change from that reception lunch when he hadn't been able to miss the way she had leaned into his cousin, Jorge, practically draping herself around the poor boy and hanging on to his every word as though he actually had something other to talk about than football.

'I just didn't think it was right for you to walk out with such an unfair impression of me.' Now that the moment had arrived, Jude discovered that she was dragging her feet, dreading when she had to tell him about her pregnancy.

'Okay. I've had a chance to get to know your friend and I would be lying if I said that I could imagine the pair of you plotting to do anything. Are you satisfied now? It's rare for me to be wrong about anything or anyone, but in this instance I may have reacted in fury. Don't forget you were the one who contrived to keep something very important a secret.'

'So did Freddy,' she pointed out, fiddling with her glass.

'Freddy had an ulterior motive.'

'So did I. I was being loyal.'

'You were my lover. Your loyalties should have been with me.'

'What else?'

Cesar looked up with a speared piece of calamari on the way to his mouth. 'What else…what?'

'You said that you said *one or two* things that weren't entirely accurate. Well, you've mentioned one thing. What's the other?'

He took his time with this mouthful of food, then washed it down with some of the white wine. He had drunk nothing at lunch and the cold wine tasted good, especially when combined with his improving spirits.

'I was enraged by what I considered your deception. I obviously still am, don't get me wrong. However, I don't consider you a gold-digger, not that I would sell my soul on that certainty. Face it, if you could lie once, you could lie a thousand times, but from what I've seen of you, I don't think you are capable of using Freddy for his money. There. Consider your character suitably exonorated, an excellent basis for civil conversation between us in the future.'

'Civil conversation…'

'Correct. Why?' He shoved aside the plate and leaned back in his chair so that he could look her squarely in the face. 'Were you expecting more?'

Something akin to pleasure raced through his veins, making this unexpected meeting well worth the temporary inconvenience. For starters, he was enjoying her company, much as he didn't care to admit it, even to himself. He wasn't too big to acknowledge that she had had more of an effect on him than he had anticipated when he had walked out of her house.

That said, of course he wasn't going to take her back. He

had offered her a chance for involvement and she had blown it. Furthermore, she had proved to be a traitor.

However, he wasn't going to deny that there was something satisfying about knowing that she was ready to come crawling back. Doubtless she had had time to really think about what he had said and ponder the truth, which was that isolating yourself from all contact with the opposite sex on the off chance that the right guy would come along with a ring in his hand and a marriage proposal on his lips was sheer lunacy. Dreams were all well and good but not when they interfered with day-to-day existence. Hell, *he'd* never had much time for idle dreaming, had he?

For a passing moment, the image of his brother flashed into his mind—his brother laughing with Imogen as they'd cut that little wedding cake at the reception. His eyes had been tender, loving, *besotted* and she had been smiling back at him with a similar expression.

'No, of course not,' she was saying awkwardly. 'Why would I expect more?'

'No idea, because there's nothing more on the table.' He signalled for the bill. Was it his imagination or did something resembling anxiety shadow her face?

'Look, this is difficult for me but there's something I need to tell you.'

Cesar stilled, sensing a level of urgency in her voice that went beyond some simple desire for them to try and *get along* for the sake of convenience. She was also fiddling like mad with the linen napkin on the table, although when she caught him noticing the nervous gesture she immediately stopped and placed her hands on her lap.

'Go on, although I haven't got all evening.'

'No.' She remembered that he probably had a date with a

leggy blonde or some other model-type creature. He had pointedly refrained from telling her exactly what he had to do later which, in her head, could only mean one thing.

'Do you remember…at the cottage? When we…made love…?'

The question came from nowhere and, taken aback, Cesar frowned. 'Of course I remember, although I thought that we were both going to pretend that that had never happened.'

'I *did* say that at the time, didn't I…'

'Have you since discovered that *selective amnesia* is a little harder to do?'

'Virtually impossible.'

'So you don't want anything more than for us to just sit here chewing the fat…but by your own admission, you can't get me out of your head…'

'It's not as clear-cut as that… I don't know quite how to say this and you're probably not going to like it but…Cesar, I'm pregnant.'

Cesar froze. The silence between them was so bottomless that, even with the dull clatter of noise around them, Jude felt that she would have been able to hear a pin drop.

'You're kidding, right,' he said finally, but his voice was raw and he had gone slightly ashen.

'I'd never kid about something like that.'

'How do you know?'

'Because I did a test two days ago. In fact, I did the test three times. Those tests are pretty much one hundred per cent accurate.'

'You can't be. You asked me if I remembered when we made love at your cottage. I do and I distinctly remember you telling me that you were protected.'

'Yes, I know and I thought I was. I really did. I mean, I

worked out when my period was due and I should have been perfectly safe but…'

Cesar was in a state of shock. When she had told him that they needed to talk, he hadn't known what to expect. It hadn't been this. Was that why she had been so desperate to know whether he had really believed her capable of using his brother? Because really she had needed to find out whether he thought her capable of using *him*?

'Was this deliberate?' he felt obliged to ask because nothing could be taken on trust, but he knew the answer already from the look on her face.

'Of course not!' Jude told him fiercely. 'Don't you think I was as shocked as you are now when I…when I did that test?' She felt her eyes threaten to fill up again but she blinked the tears away and clenched her fists.

'Okay. I believe you.'

She felt a wave of relief. From the various scenarios which had played in her head, most had featured an accusing and disbelieving Cesar, who saw her as someone who had intruded into his life and, having infiltrated, had used the situation to her own advantage.

At least that nasty possibility was out of the way, leaving her to face the stark reality, which was that she and Cesar no longer shared an intimate connection, that she had only ever been a sex object to him, easily and quickly disposable. Now that she was pregnant, nothing was destined to change but they would have to work out some sort of civil arrangement whereby they could deal with the situation.

In all her girlhood dreams, being pregnant by a man who didn't love her had never featured. Plan A had always been to have children in a loving relationship. She now had to face some pretty harsh facts. She was on Plan B and she would just have to deal with it.

'I haven't come here to ask anything of you,' she told him quietly. 'I'm pretty realistic.' She smiled sadly. 'We had a very brief fling but there's nothing between us now so we just need to sort out…well, what happens when the baby is born…'

'What do you mean, *what happens*?'

'About…visiting…I know it's early days but…it's probably better to deal with things now…or at least discuss them… I know this is a bombshell…'

'That has to be the understatement of the year.'

'Anyway, perhaps I could give you a few days to think about things, let it sink in…?'

'Let it sink in? It's already sunk in!' He raked restless fingers through his hair and looked at her, imagining *his* baby in her tummy. Fatherhood had never been something he had contemplated. In fact, the concept was completely alien to both his way of thinking and his lifestyle.

'Nothing has to change for you,' she said quickly. 'This is *my* situation.'

'*Your* situation? What planet are you on, Jude? Whether you like it or not, this is fifty per cent *my* doing.'

'But it's my fault that I'm pregnant. I wasn't careful enough. I should have thought.'

'It's pointless debating whose fault it is or isn't. Right now we need to get out of here, go somewhere where we can talk privately.' He stood up and beckoned for the bill at the same time. 'My apartment's just round the corner. We'll go there.'

CHAPTER EIGHT

CESAR'S apartment was literally a five-minute walk away. It made sense to be out of the restaurant, to go somewhere more private to talk, but Jude still felt nervous as they walked along in silence, she huddling into her coat while he seemed lost in his thoughts.

She reminded herself that he had now moved on from her, which made her think of his ruined date. The poor blonde was probably waiting at some table in some unknown restaurant, checking her watch and tapping her long scarlet fingernails impatiently as it dawned on her that she might have been stood up. Jude didn't feel at all sorry about that. In fact, the thought provided her with a few moments of well-deserved amusement.

'We're here.'

She snapped out of her pleasant daydream and looked up at the sharp, clear lines of a four-storey Georgian town house with its neat black railings fringed by two impeccably groomed shrubs. It reeked of money and the impression was cemented by the array of flashy cars parked on either side of the wide street. Even in the darkness, this was clearly a part of London reserved for the immensely wealthy, a far cry from the cheap and cheerful hotel room she had reserved for herself for the overnight stay.

Inside, the large flagstoned hall was dotted with yet more well-manicured plants and she followed him to the lift, which took them up two flights to his apartment, which occupied the upper floors of the building. Two complete floors!

Jude looked around her for a while, forgetting the seriousness of the situation that had brought her to this place.

The floors were pale blond wood and here, on the lower of the floors, was the sitting area, the kitchen and several other rooms which she could only glimpse. Up a curving iron staircase were the bedrooms and bathrooms, how many she had no idea. It was incredibly neat and clean and had the perfect appearance of a place that would not disgrace the cover of a house magazine.

'Nice place,' Jude said politely. She tentatively made her way to one of the sprawling cream leather sofas but was hesitant to sit on it.

'It won't bite,' Cesar said drily. 'It's only a piece of furniture.' The bracing night air had taken some of the edge from his initial shock. He wouldn't go down that road of thinking just how his life was going to change. There were so many areas to contemplate that it seemed better to scrap the thought altogether. The main thing was that he was going to be a father and pondering the consequences wasn't going to get him anywhere. 'I'm getting myself a cup of coffee. Do you want one?'

'Thank you. No. I think I've probably had more than my fair ration today.'

Her eyes strayed to the huge abstract paintings on the walls and the weird pieces of sculpture that had been artistically positioned on the mantelpiece of what was a very modern fireplace.

She looked back at him as he sat on one of the low matching leather chairs facing her.

'I'm sorry.' If she hadn't realised how much this was going

to upset his life, then being in his apartment was a lesson in finding out because it reflected *him*, the man. Here was a person with no use for clutter or lack of order, two things that followed in the wake of a child. 'I've given this some thought,' she said hesitantly, 'and I've worked out that you won't have your life disrupted. No, please, Cesar...' This when he was about to interrupt. 'I can take care of the baby on my own and, naturally, you can visit whenever you want to or whenever you have the time...'

'Visit whenever I want...? When I have time...? We're not talking about an art gallery here, Jude. We're talking about a child—*my* child.'

'Well, yes, I realise that...'

Cesar sipped his coffee and continued to look at her while she, in turn, stared miserably at the intricately weaved Persian rug under her feet.

'I'm not sure you do,' Cesar countered. 'No, my parental rights will go way beyond occasional visits when you give the go-ahead. For starters, there's the question of money. You might like to think yourself not materialistic but no child of mine is ever going to endure any kind of hardship. Both your future and the future of my child will be secure. Of that you have my word.'

He allowed several seconds of silence to elapse, giving her time to absorb what he was saying.

'Hardship? Cesar, I have a job! I know I may not earn what you consider sufficient to live on, but your idea of an adequate amount of money is...well, completely different to most people's...' She looked round the apartment. The paintings on his walls probably cost as much as most people's holidays abroad. More. 'This isn't real life!'

'Agreed, but this is *my* life and it's the life my child will enjoy.'

'What are you trying to say?' She unconsciously rested her hand on her stomach as the colour drained from her face. This was something she hadn't considered. What if he decided that he wanted the child? Wanted to fight for sole custody of her baby? Would he do that? 'You won't take my baby away from me!'

'Of course I am not going to take your baby away from you!' Cesar was genuinely appalled at the suggestion. 'What sort of man do you think I am? I realise the need for a child to have its mother, to have *both* its parents, which brings me to the point I'm trying to make.'

Jude nodded, half listening to him, sagging with relief that she had jumped the gun for no reason.

'...so you see, whilst I am prepared to put financial security on the table, a child needs more than just that. As you have said a dozen times, it's not all about money...'

'Right.'

'And having both parents around means more than me driving to Kent once a week for a three-hour visit. When I say that I intend to be there for my child, I mean it. I intend to be there on a permanent basis, as in living on the premises. With you. With our child. Together. A unit. Married.'

It took Jude a few seconds to process that information, then she replayed it in her head just to make sure that she wasn't imagining that word, *married*.

'Are you telling me that you want to *get married*? *To me?*' Jude laughed incredulously. 'That's the most ridiculous thing I've ever heard in my life.'

Cesar stiffened. 'No child of mine will be born out of wedlock.'

'*Born out of wedlock?* Cesar, this is the twenty-first century! In case you hadn't noticed, pregnancy and marriage no

longer necessarily go together! Besides, isn't it a bit hypocriti-
cal to say something like that when you were prepared to bend
the rules for your brother?'

'I was prepared *to protect my brother at all costs from
someone I thought might be using him for his money.* Different
thing. Anyway, we're getting off topic here.' He stood up and
began pacing the room until he finally stopped directly in front
of her, then he sat on the sofa next to her so that she had to
propel herself back a couple of inches to stop herself from
falling against him.

'Surely you have to concede that a two-parent family is
superior to a one-parent one.'

'Yes, *in an ideal world*, but we're not living in an *ideal
world*, Cesar.' In an ideal world, there was nothing Jude would
have wanted more than to have been asked to be Cesar's wife
and for a couple of wild seconds she was ashamed to find
herself buying into a beguiling fantasy picture in her head of
a family of three, blissfully happy, doing normal family
things. It didn't last long.

'Why would you ask me to marry you, Cesar?'

'Isn't it obvious?' He frowned. Okay, so all of this had
come as a complete shock to him but he was now doing the
honourable thing and, in his head, the *only* thing and, instead
of fairly leaping at all the benefits being thrown on the table,
she had firstly laughed at him and now seemed to be asking
him for accountability on his offer.

'Cesar—' she sighed '—you can't just marry someone
because she happens to be pregnant with your child and then
assume that it'll all work out fine. We weren't even going out
together! Would you be sitting here with me *at all* if this
hadn't happened?'

'That's not the point.'

'But it *is* the point.' She could see that, having made the ultimate sacrifice and proposed marriage, it hadn't occurred to him that his offer might be rejected. 'Did you ever think about getting married again? Starting a family? No, don't answer that because I already know the answer and it's no.'

'Things have changed…I've never been in this position before…'

'And there's no need to put a ring on my finger because you *are*…' Jude wondered whether she was being crazy. She loved him! She could think of nothing greater than going to bed with him at night and waking up to him in the morning, and if she were married to him, he might just come to love her after a while. Relationships were things that were built gradually over time, weren't they? Each brick going down making it stronger and more durable.

But what if it didn't work out that way?

The voice of realism stole into her head and swept aside all her romantic illusions. It wasn't an ideal world after all and a man trapped in a marriage soon became a resentful man, even if he had built the trap himself and willingly jumped in. Cesar had grown accustomed to a life of freedom. How long would it take before he wanted that freedom back?

'I know you think you're doing the right thing,' she said gently, 'but my answer has to be no.'

'It isn't just about the child,' he told her roughly. 'I…I still want you…'

'But I may not want *you*…'

'Shall we put that to the test?' He curled his fingers into her hair and pulled her towards him, unleashing all the cravings she had been storing up ever since he had walked out of her house.

Jude shuddered against him as his mouth crushed hers, hot and urgent and demanding.

She was trembling as he swept her off the sofa and carried her to his bedroom. When he laid her on his bed, she began sitting up, gathering the strength to walk away, but her mouth dried as she watched him pull off his clothes, revealing bit by bit that wonderful body that had haunted her dreams.

Yes, he wanted her. Still. The proof was there in front of her eyes and, while this had nothing to do with love, it was so powerful that she gave a little groan of despair. Her feet were dangling off the bed and she still had on the high-heeled pumps, which she now kicked off.

He disposed of her dress in one swift, easy movement and then her tights, which were tossed on the ground to join the chaos of discarded clothes.

When he nuzzled against her lacy bra, Jude whimpered and ran her fingers along his shoulders. She could trace every muscle and sinew. She arched her spine so that her rosebud nipples pushed against the constricting fabric and then closed her eyes as he pulled aside the bra, allowing her breasts to push free.

Already, her breasts were becoming more tender with the pregnancy. Now, the feel of his tongue delicately licking the tautened bud was achingly pleasurable and she wanted it never to stop.

She half opened her eyes, watching that dark arrogant head as he devoted all his attention to teasing her and it was a massive turn-on.

As he continued to lick first one sensitive nipple before moving on to the next, he ran his hand along her body, over her still flat stomach and then down to her matching lacy briefs, where he tantalised her by allowing his fingers to rest there just for a moment before slipping his hand under the cloth so that he could play with her.

Every inch of her body screamed with wanting him to take

her but he was being wonderfully, maddeningly gentle as he continued to suckle on her while teasing her moistness with his fingers.

In a gesture of thrilling intimacy, he slowly made his way downwards and kissed her stomach, fluttery little kisses that had her spellbound, then farther down, he carried on kissing her and finally parting that aching place so that he could drive her crazy with his tongue.

Jude arched up to meet that exploring mouth and writhed against him as the sensations he was unlocking started coming quicker and quicker.

By day she had replayed in her head the harshness of his parting words, using it as a tool for self-protection, but by night this was what she had dreamed of—the slide of his tongue in her, the feel of his hands roaming over her body, possessively claiming it as his own. She had the weird sensation that she was living a dream.

She heard her own disembodied voice crying out his name as he thrust into her, taking her with sure, slow strokes that sent her wild.

It was a while before those waves of pleasure finally peaked and subsided, leaving her spent.

'We're good together,' Cesar murmured. On his side now, he pulled her into him. 'You tell me that you don't want to marry me, but at the bottom of every successful marriage is a foundation of passion, and you can't deny that there's passion between us.'

'I'm not denying it, Cesar.' She placed her hands squarely on his chest and created some distance between them. She was feverishly trying to work out how she had succumbed to him, but she didn't have to look far for the answer. If she hadn't loved him she would have had the strength to be indifferent to his advances. She certainly would have had the strength to have realised that climbing into bed with him was one sure way of undermining her resolve.

They both had the baby to consider and sleeping with Cesar was sure to complicate matters.

'But it doesn't mean that I'm going to marry you for all the wrong reasons.' She spun onto her side and was getting out of the bed when he pulled her back to face him.

'We're not doing this again!' he grated. 'Pretending that nothing happened just then. You're just going to have to wake up to the fact that we enjoy making love.'

'I haven't said that we don't! I'm just saying that it was a mistake.'

'Really? That's not what your body was saying when I was touching it.'

'Cesar, it's not enough and I think I should be going now. I've said what I wanted to say. There's no reason why we have to meet again, at least not until it's closer to the date and then we can discuss everything in more detail.' She wriggled off the bed and began hunting down her clothes, feeling very exposed.

When she looked over her shoulder, it was to find him propped up on one elbow, watching her.

'You need someone to take care of you.'

'I'm pregnant! I'm not ill!'

'And living in the middle of nowhere isn't very convenient for me.'

'Guess what, Cesar. This isn't about what's convenient for you and what isn't.' Dress now on, she stood up and fished her shoes out from under his trousers.

'You can't get back on your own.' He sprang out of bed and hastily began putting on his clothes.

This had turned out to be one hell of a day. In fact, the past couple of months would go down on record as the most life-changing he had ever experienced. He was finding it more and more difficult to remember the tranquillity of his brief marriage to Marisol. That time almost seemed unreal. Sugary and unreal—nothing like the grittiness of what he had recently been put through.

'Of course I can!'

'I don't intend to disappear until you think it's time to summon me back on the scene!'

'I'm not asking you to disappear!' She turned around to find him standing right behind her. 'But everything's going to be just a matter of routine for the next few months!'

'I will have to break this news to the public at large, including my family in Spain. My *very orthodox* family. What am I supposed to tell them? That I'm going to have a baby but the mother doesn't want anything to do with me?'

'Is that what this is all about? Appealing to convention?'

'There's nothing wrong with convention.'

Cesar was baffled and enraged that, even after making love, even after confessing that she still wanted him as much as he wanted her, she continued to dig her heels in. She wanted a knight in shining armour? Was he not that knight in shining armour, promising her a ring on her finger and a lifetime of ease? She would never have to worry about money, would be able to devote herself solely and entirely to the raising of their child. How many men, confronted with an unplanned pregnancy, would have done as much? It all seemed to make sense to him but yet again he was discovering that nothing made sense where this woman was involved.

Presented with a problem, he'd come up with a solution and a pretty damned good one, but not good enough, apparently.

'Where are you staying?' He shoved on his shoes, minus the

socks because she was already flying to the door when she should have been lying in his arms, still languorous from making love and looking forward to making love all over again.

She gave him the name of her hotel, one which was unfamiliar to him but, judging from the sound of its location, not one in which the mother of his unborn child should be staying and he told her so.

Jude flashed him a look that gave him her answer. From being a block of ice at the wedding, he had now become rampantly over-protective and solicitous and it would have been amusing if it hadn't been so sad. He had probably thought that enticing her back between the sheets would have softened her up, that she would have reconsidered and decided that yes, she was willing to have a marriage of convenience because it was what tradition demanded. As far as he was concerned, they would get married so that the dishonour of having an illegitimate child was avoided and have a sexual relationship until such time as he got tired of her, because lust only had a short lifespan before it faded away into boredom. And then she would stay at home, enjoying all the things that his money could buy her, while he had his discreet affairs. He would respect her as the mother of his child but he would never love her as a woman and as his wife. That was not one of the things he was willing to put on the table.

'Okay, I'll drive you there myself but it's not suitable. I have connections at some of the best hotels in London. I could get you a room at any one of them.'

'I don't want a room at any one of them!'

'Why the hell do you have to be so stubborn?' She was at the door now and, more than anything else, he just wanted to scoop her up and carry her back to his king-sized bed, where he could keep an eye on her because it seemed that the minute she was out of his sight, he lost control of his life. Hadn't that been the case for the past three weeks? Even seeing her earlier at the wedding had unsettled him, had distracted him from the business of his brother getting married. How the hell was he going to face the prospect of her, pregnant with his child, *doing her own thing*?

'I'm stubborn? Honestly, Cesar, you should take a look in the mirror. You're the most stubborn man in the world! You just won't take *no* for an answer!'

'I'm trying to be practical…and you have to be willing to compromise…'

'I *am* compromising. I came and told you, didn't I? I could very well have decided to keep you out of the loop. I *could* have sloped off and had the baby and you would have been none the wiser.'

'That wouldn't be your style, Jude. You're far too honest for that. Besides, where would you have sloped off *to*? And don't you think that Fernando and Imogen would have been a little curious when you started putting on weight? Anyway…I accept that you might want to go away and think about what I have asked…'

'Remember what I said about your stubbornness and inability to take *no* for an answer?' But as they walked towards the car she had to smile to herself.

'Believe me, you're only now discovering just how stubborn I can be.' Already Cesar was thinking about the situation and coming up with a fresh strategy. She wasn't prepared to marry him…*yet*…but he would still need to be around. He wasn't going to settle for doing a vanishing act until he got a phone call at three in the morning telling him that he was a father.

Besides…and in the darkness of the car, his eyes slid over to her neat profile…it had been disconcertingly easy to take this bombshell in his stride. Of course, he was a man capable of dealing with pretty much anything that life had to throw at him because, with the exception of health problems, there was nothing that could not be sorted out with a cool head, but he found himself a lot less disturbed by the notion of parenthood than he might have expected.

'Okay—' Cesar raised his shoulders in a gesture that indicated magnanimity in defeat '—for the moment I will accept that you have reservations about my offer. Although,' he couldn't help adding, 'I don't understand why, but I don't want to argue with you. Now is not a time for arguing.'

'No, it's not.' After all the tension of the past couple of days and the past couple of hours, Jude gave in to a moment of wickedness. 'After all, I *am* pregnant, and pregnant women shouldn't argue. Something about stress being bad for the baby…'

Cesar swerved the car over to the pavement and stopped. 'Is that what the doctor told you?'

'Why have you stopped?'

'Because I won't be accused of doing anything that might jeopardise this pregnancy.'

'Cesar, I was joking!' She looked at him, surprised at his reaction. 'Are you trying to tell me that you're *glad* that I'm pregnant?'

'I'm trying to tell you that…you shouldn't stress…' Put on the spot, Cesar was not going to commit himself to saying anything that might be misconstrued. *Glad* was a pretty big word. 'I'm here and I can take anything in my stride.'

'Oh.' Jude couldn't hide her disappointment. He had taken all this a lot better than she had expected, but then he had been put in an unenviable position and maybe, having resigned himself to the inevitable, he *was* now getting used to the idea of having a child. Maybe, just maybe, even *liking* it. But that didn't mean that he was pleased that *she* happened to be the mother. Like he said, he was just taking it all in his stride.

'But if *I* can take this in my stride and accommodate it into my life, then I feel that *you* should be prepared to meet me halfway.' That little word *glad* was still niggling somewhere at the back of his brain, in the same place, in fact, where he had stored away the explosive notion that he had been *missing* something in his life. It was just an unsettling feeling he had had seeing his brother, Imogen and their baby and, unused to dealing with anything less than complete satisfaction with the path he had chosen for himself, he had opted to shelve the feeling rather than deal with it. 'And I mean *literally* halfway.'

'Is this suggestion going to stress me out?' Jude asked lightly.

'No. In fact…' Cesar looked at her with a certain amount of self-satisfaction '…the opposite. It's going to make your life a lot easier and it'll give me peace of mind.' He started the engine and pulled away from the kerb, back on course to her hotel. 'I want you closer to me,' he said. It felt strange to say something like that to a woman but he let it go. These were exceptional circumstances. 'I'm a traditionalist. You know that and you're just going to have to run with it.'

Jude sighed, indulging his arrogance, which was so much part and parcel of the person he was.

'The mother of my child can't be allowed to run wild in the back of beyond, refusing all offers of help from me through sheer pride.'

Given such an array of misconceptions, Jude struggled to find one in particular on which she could latch. *'Run wild?'*

'I can see you know where I'm coming from.' Up ahead was her hotel, which wasn't the run-down one-star Cesar had imagined. In fact, he had to admit that it looked perfectly all right, although nowhere near the standard he was used to. Next to him, Jude seemed to be struggling to say something.

'*Back of beyond?*'

'I give you *snowbound.*'

'*Sheer pride?*'

'You said it. I see we're on the same wavelength here, which is a good thing because…' *you're going to move.* Cesar nearly said it but remembered in time that that phraseology would be like waving a red rag to a bull and right now tact was called for. '…I think it would be an immensely good idea if you move a bit closer to me. I'm not saying central London. I realise you have your work out there, but correct me if I am wrong—you freelance, so you could work from anywhere, right?'

'Yes, but…'

'Thought so. You could easily rent your cottage. Holiday let of some sort. People are always wanting to have weekend breaks in the middle of nowhere, for reasons I, personally, have never understood. So you let your cottage and I buy you somewhere a bit closer, somewhere I can actually get to quickly without having to use the company helicopter. There are some extremely pleasant areas around London that boast accessible road and rail links.'

Jude opened her mouth to inform him of the ease of transport from her cottage in most weather conditions, that she had furnished that cottage from scratch and it was her pride and joy and that he could take a running jump if he thought that he could manoeuvre her into his point of view just because he happened to be something of a dinosaur when it came to this unique situation. Instead, she said faintly, 'You can't just *buy* me a house.'

'Why not?' They were at the hotel and he parked his Bentley and turned toward her.

'Because people don't *do* stuff like that.'

'I thought we'd already established that I'm not like other people. Anyway, you are entitled. What do you look for in a house?'

Jude, who had no intention of accepting any such thing, was nevertheless distracted by the thought of *his* house—all modern flooring, expensive rugs and uncomfortable leather furniture that was designed to be displayed rather than sat on.

'Certainly not anything like yours,' she said and he gave her a disarming grin that sent her pulses racing.

'What's wrong with my apartment?'

'I hate leather furniture. It's too cold in winter and sticks to your legs in summer. And wooden flooring should be authentic. And paintings of lines and circles don't make any sense.'

'Anything else?'

'And don't you miss having a garden? Some small square patch of lawn? Somewhere you can sit in summer with a glass of wine?'

'No. What else do you hate about my apartment?'

'Sorry.' Too late now for an apology, she supposed, but while he seemed so open to criticism, she couldn't help adding, 'It doesn't look *lived in*.' She wondered what his house with his wife had looked like. Had it had a woman's touch? Flowers in vases? Recipe books bought with optimism but destined to sit on shelves in the kitchen unopened? Pictures of family members in frames? 'What was your house like in Spain when you were married?'

Cesar frowned. He hadn't really thought of that before. He had thought about Marisol, had put her in a safe keeping place in his mind, but the house? When he thought of a house, he thought of Jude's house—its casual warmth, the cosy clutter, the log fire burning in the sitting room.

'Big, as a matter of fact.' He should really let her go now, into her hotel, but it was comfortable being in the dark car with her. He rationalised that this was all part of the process of establishing an easier relationship with her. She was no longer just a woman with whom he had had a brief fling and who had caused him to lose a bit of sleep by bruising his ego. She was much more important than that now. He had a *duty* to sit here with her, to talk, to watch those fascinating expressions flit across her face, ambushing all her hopes of ever being mysterious and unreadable.

'I can't remember how many bedrooms…or sitting rooms, for that matter. Lots of marble.'

'Wow. Very grand.' Of course that would be his preferred taste in houses.

'Very grand,' Cesar agreed. 'A present from her parents.'

'Useful parents.' Jude laughed ruefully. 'Although I think I rather like the thought of small and cosy.'

'I know.'

'Anyway,' she said briskly, before his fond trip down memory lane had her bursting into tears, 'I'll be gone now. I feel exhausted.' She yawned as tiredness threatened to overwhelm her. She remembered what he had said about wanting her closer to him but suddenly she felt too weary to reopen the debate. Also, it wouldn't hurt to have just one night to indulge her romantic notions and wallow in the warmth of him telling her that he wanted to marry her, wanted her *as his wife*, that, failing that, he wanted her close to him. She would leave reality out of it and just pick the bits and pieces of his conversation that she wanted to hear. What was the harm in that? She would call him in the morning and tell him that having a house bought for her was entirely out of the question and he would have to play by *her* rules.

* * *

Three days later and Jude was still trying to get through to Cesar, who was, according to his secretary, out of the office closing a deal. Nor was he attainable on his mobile, which really brought home to her once and for all that her fragile, spun glass, you're-the-mother-of-my-child status was a figment of her imagination. All that mattered to Cesar was his work. It took priority over everything. As she was sitting in front of her bowl of cereal, idly thinking about what she had to do but mostly rehearsing what she would say to Cesar when she finally managed to get hold of him, she was jolted out of her thoughts by the sharp sound of her doorbell.

She opened the door with her cup of tea in her hand and there he was, materialising yet again out of thin air and making her wonder whether it was physically possible to summon someone up just by thinking very hard about them.

Jude's treacherous heart skipped a beat. At seven-thirty in the morning he looked gut-wrenchingly handsome and she scowled, remembering her frustrated efforts to get through to him.

'What are you doing here?' she demanded. 'I've been trying to get hold of you!'

'Is that *all* you ever wear?' Cesar eyed the shapeless dungarees with gleaming eyes.

'Where *were* you?' Jude repeated in a shrill voice.

'Important stuff. You'll have to go and get changed into something more…less utilitarian.'

'Why? I'm not going anywhere with you!'

'And forget about being stubborn. There's something you need to see.'

CHAPTER NINE

'IS THIS the deal I was told you were working on?'

They had just finished walking around the house which Cesar had threatened to buy and which Jude had spent the past three days deciding against, with her refusal becoming more eloquent in her head the longer she had tried to reach him by phone and failed.

It had taken them less than an hour to make it to the small hamlet on the outskirts of London, during which time he had pointedly refused to tell her the reason for his sudden urgency to take her out, instead keeping the conversation light. Every time she had tried to bring the subject back to the speech she had rehearsed, he had danced round her remarks and told her that he would talk seriously once they were out of the car and he could concentrate fully on what she was saying. As if he ever had the slightest difficulty in multi-tasking.

And now here they were.

He had clearly paid a great deal of attention to every word she had said about his apartment because there was an ostensible absence of anything modern in the house, although Jude could tell at a glance that everything was of a superbly high standard. The country-style kitchen with its small green Aga and the four-poster bed with its patchwork quilt—exquisite and no expense spared.

'This is the deal I was working on,' Cesar agreed, his dark eyes raking intently over her face. He had had to move at the speed of light but, with a bottomless pit of money at his disposal, Cesar had had no trouble in locating the ideal house in the ideal village which was within ideal driving distance of both his work and his apartment.

'Just look around before you say anything,' he had told her the minute he had seen the protestations rising to her lips. 'If you don't like the idea then I'll respect your decision.' He had banked on the house doing his work for him by wooing her and, although he wasn't certain of success, he was sure he had a better chance of her agreeing to this concession than he had three days ago when she had turned down his marriage proposal flat.

She had made all the right noises at the small, attractive mature garden with its own little orchard with apple and plum trees, had paused to admire the rough old beams in the house, the open fireplace with the date engraved on the mantelpiece and its border of original Victorian tiles, had run her hands over the Aga, which kept the place beautifully warm, and had admitted to him in the bedroom that she had always wanted a four-poster bed.

Cesar could feel triumph vibrating in the air between them. 'Well,' he asked pleasantly, 'what do you think of it? Do you like it?'

'Who wouldn't?'

They had retired to the kitchen and were now facing one another across the pine table, in the centre of which was a vase of wild flowers.

'It's the right distance from central London,' Cesar said,

working his sales pitch carefully because experience had taught him that one errant word would have her scuttling into defence mode. He still couldn't quite grasp why and how she could have seen his marriage proposal as some sort of insult. He had offered her the highest prize and she had rejected it but there was nothing to be gained from dwelling on that. 'And it's a commutable distance from where you are now. You could easily make it back if you need to for work purposes, or to visit friends…'

Temptation dangled in front of her eyes. Cesar didn't love her but he was driven to take care of her because she was carrying his baby. Of course, she would never, ever marry him for all the reasons she had told herself over and over again, but it was kind of comforting to know that he could be *right there* should she ever have the need to call on him and *right there* when their child was born and he wanted to visit.

'I could buy the house today,' he said, his dark velvety voice seducing her. 'The owners have moved to the Far East and they're willing to sell the furniture or what bits of it you might want… You could move in by the end of next week…' He allowed that cosy image to form in her head.

'We haven't even *discussed* this!' Jude objected. 'It's crazy for you to think that you can just go and find me somewhere else to live because it suits you, without even bothering to consult me!'

'Would you have agreed to go on a house hunt with me?'

'Maybe not but that's not the point.'

'Of course it's the point. You would keep putting obstacles in the way and making life as difficult as you possibly could for me. I made a managerial decision and chose the option that would suit us both.'

'I'm not one of your employees, Cesar! Someone you can boss around and give orders to!'

'I wouldn't consider buying a house for any of my employees. Now you've seen this place, tell me what you don't like about it.'

'It's not about *the house*. Of course I like the house! I've already told you so. It's about the *presumption*.'

'You mean the presumption that I might want a situation that works in some small measure for me as well as for you. So you like the house, it's in a brilliant location. So your real objection is that you wanted to have the opportunity to dig your heels in and exercise your right of refusal. You are carrying my baby and now that you have that leverage to blackmail, you intend to use it to the fullest. Is that it?'

'Of course it isn't.' Jude gave him a sulky look because, put like that, he somehow made her sound petty.

'And I don't *dig my heels in*,' she continued and Cesar raised his eyebrows in blatant incredulity. 'There's a difference between *digging your heels in* and *having an opinion*,' she carried on, her mouth downturned.

'Give me a concrete objection, Jude, and spare me the postulating.'

'I have heaps of stuff in my cottage…'

'Transporting whatever you wanted to bring could be done in the snap of a finger…'

'But moving house is a really big deal. Anyway, I can't let you *buy* this for me…'

'Could you let me buy it for my child?' Cesar shrugged because the whole matter of finance was immaterial to him. The cost of the house was an infinitesimal drop in the ocean for him. 'If you like, the house can remain in my name, held in trust for our child. These small concerns barely matter.'

Jude heard the sound of arguments forming in her head and being washed away by the ebb and flow of Cesar's logic and determination.

And her own clawing love for him was undermining all her objections. She liked the sound of his familiar drawl, thrilled to the prospect of knowing that he was within easy reach, was guiltily aware that she really craved the thought of being the sole focus of his attentiveness at least for a few months, even though the short-term fix would probably do even more long-term damage to her mental state.

'Well…' She drew the syllable out and Cesar knew that he had won. She would move in. He was surprised at how relieved he felt at that thought.

'I still don't much like the idea of accepting this…' Jude felt obliged to point out because she wasn't about to be brow-beaten on all fronts '…but I guess I can compromise and then, when the baby's born, we can take it from there…'

'Whatever you say.'

In actual fact, it was a little over a fortnight later when Jude moved her final set of project designs into the house and during that time she had found it hard to cling onto her picture of Cesar as the arrogant man who only wanted her because of an accident of circumstance, a man who would just as soon set her up as his wife as he would leave her to her own devices the minute he got bored of her appeal.

She had to constantly remind herself that the voice which had guided her away from accepting something that should never be offered without love was the voice that should be heeded, because Cesar was on the charm offensive. He phoned her, helped her sort out the rental of her cottage, single-handedly made sure that every stick she wanted to take with her was duly transported. She had no idea what havoc this was wreaking with his precious work life but when she tried to ask he waved aside her questions as though they were an irrelevance. In the end, Jude gave up. She accepted his presence and kept to herself just how pleasurable she found it being in his company, especially like this, when they weren't arguing.

They also weren't in any way *touching*.

He greeted her with a careful peck on the cheek and said goodbye in the same way. It made Jude feel like an inanimate object, one which he was duty-bound to protect, though not so treasured that he was inclined to caress.

He had pressed the fast forward button on the physical attraction part of their relationship and arrived at that place which she had foreseen slightly further down the line. Instead of feeling more justified in knowing that she had done the right thing in turning him down, she just felt horribly hollow and empty.

A week after she'd moved in, she gave in to the perverse desire to put this to the test.

Cesar had phoned her earlier in the day and told her that he would be taking her out to dinner. Dinner with Cesar invariably involved a very expensive restaurant. Making do with what happened to be lying about in the kitchen was no more than a fond memory of two days snatched in her cottage when a lack of choice had seen him play at domesticity.

He showed up at the house promptly at seven. He must have quit work at a ridiculous hour, especially considering it was Friday, the day before the rest of the world rested, when he was inclined to work long into the night on anything that couldn't survive a weekend break. He was, tellingly, no longer in his work gear. The weather had improved steadily over the weeks and he was in a pair of jeans that lovingly moulded his muscular legs and a navy-blue jumper, the cost of which was only apparent in the very small logo on one side.

'I've decided to cook something,' Jude said, leading him through to the sitting room, into which she had brought all her mementoes from the cottage, but retained the furniture that had been left there.

'I can smell it. Why?'

'Don't you ever get tired of eating out?'

'It's a lifestyle that's grown on me over the years. Have you seen my brother recently? He is beginning to look like a married man.'

This was the Cesar he had become, someone who could charmingly talk about anything and everything, but without the passion that had driven him in their past fraught encounters. Over the meal she had prepared, he chatted amicably about Freddy and the jazz club, which was due for its big opening night in three months. Already the signs were that it wouldn't take long to break even and then would prove to have been a profitable investment.

Cesar, typically, was not averse to some self-promotion on this front but laughed when she gave him a knowing look from under her lashes.

'Okay!' He raised his hands in mock surrender. 'You can't shoot a guy for trying.'

Jude started to clear the table and said casually, 'Do you think that I'm beginning to look fat?' She offered her profile for his inspection, knowing that her bump was there but still small, although her breasts had grown.

After his sarcastic remark about her very practical dungarees, she had put them aside for a while and was in a pair of black fitted trousers and a black long-sleeved jersey top with tiny buttons halfway down the front.

She was also not wearing a bra, having grown out of her old ones but not wanting to commit to unnecessary expenditure when she might well get bigger.

Cesar drew in his breath sharply.

The past few weeks had seen him taking his time with her, behaving in a manner that was alien to him when it came to women, particularly considering he had slept with this woman and she still haunted his mind, tantalising him with the memory of her body, which was filling out now, her breasts enlarging, her once flat stomach showing signs of the baby she was carrying.

But she didn't want him, or at least not enough, and he wasn't going to rock the boat by throwing her back on the defensive. Knowing that she would probably involuntarily respond to him if he touched her was worthless knowledge. He wanted her mind to respond as well as her body because her mind would not want to sweep the physical attraction between them under the carpet where it could lie out of sight and out of mind.

'A pregnant woman cannot be classified as fat,' he said neutrally. Of course he knew that she wasn't wearing a bra. He had known it the minute he had stepped through the door. It was also pretty obvious that her breasts had expanded as well. They would now be a full handful. And her nipples, he guessed, would also have swelled with the pregnancy, swelled and darkened. He didn't want to look at that sideways view being innocently offered for his inspection, he didn't want to see the outline of those nipples with their little firm buds pressing against the fabric of her top.

'I feel fat,' Jude said lightly, running her hands over her stomach. 'I think it's because I've always been so skinny and everywhere's bigger now. Not just my stomach.'

Cesar, invited to see what those other bits were, reluctantly looked at her breasts. 'To be expected.' He was surprised to hear his voice sounding so normal. 'I guess you'll have to start investing in bigger clothes. It goes without saying that any purchases will be put on the credit card I gave you.'

Jude sighed with a mixture of frustration and resignation. Point proved. If she ripped off her clothes now he would probably warn her about the dangers of catching cold in her fragile state. Had he even noticed that she had dumped the bra?

'Have you used that card *at all*?' Cesar took refuge in the sheer boredom of talking about spending and credit cards. If she only knew the effect she had on him, she would run a mile.

'Of course I haven't!' Jude snapped. The house came with a dishwasher but she preferred the cathartic process of washing the dishes herself, which she now began to do with great vigour. 'I *am* still working, still earning my own money and, in fact, in a month's time I'll be getting a rental income from the cottage so my finances are looking healthy. No need to dip into the vast Caretti reserves just yet!'

'You throw that in my face as though it's an insult to have it at your disposal!'

Jude could think of something else that was a lot more insulting, namely the way he had politely looked at her body and then told her that weight gain was *to be expected*. It was the sort of thing her doctor might tell her before giving her a lecture on making sure to eat well and avoid alcohol.

She did quite like the idea of arguing with him because an argument would mean *heat* and *passion* of a sort, but pregnancy had mellowed her, so instead she made her peace and carried on making her peace for the remainder of the evening, which was pleasantly spent until he was ready to leave at a little after eleven.

He was going to be away for a few days from next Monday, he told her as he lounged against the door frame on his way out. Would she be able to manage?

'Of course I'll be able to manage,' Jude told him irritably. 'I keep telling you that you don't have to watch over me like a mother hen.'

'Great comparison. Guaranteed to make a man feel so virile.'

'I don't have to tell you that you're virile,' she said even more irritably. 'You know you are.'

'Oh, yes. So I am.' He reached out and touched her stomach, keeping his hand flat on the small mound, then rubbing it gently, which sent shivers of inappropriate excitement racing up and down her spine. She wondered what he would do if she grabbed his hand and pushed it under her T-shirt.

'I've bought one of those pregnancy books,' he admitted, removing his hand and sticking it into the pocket of his trousers.

'You've *bought a pregnancy book*?' Jude laughed. 'You never said. Is it your bedtime reading? I thought you went to bed with important reports and your laptop computer!'

'I've only dipped into it,' Cesar told her gruffly. 'And I would seriously advise you against reading one of those things. They're full of horror stories.'

'That's probably because you're squeamish.' Jude was still laughing at the thought of this big, dominant male reading a pregnancy manual and feeling queasy.

'You're talking to one of the least squeamish men to walk the earth. I am also incredibly robust, never a day's illness.'

'That's because you're so bossy that germs can't be bothered to attack you.'

'Things are good between us, aren't they, Jude? Admit it. We can talk like this, laugh... Tell me why you find it so damned difficult to commit to me! *I* was supposed to be the commitment-phobe.'

'Don't spoil the night, Cesar.'

And, besides…what was he committing to? Fulfilling his obligations as a prospective parent? Being a superb financial provider? Having an amicable relationship with her, one in which they would be able to behave in a civilised fashion for the sake of the child?

He would see all that as the greatest sacrifice but he didn't love her and from all appearances was no longer even physically attracted to her, which meant that he could throw out that word *commitment* as much as he liked. In the end it all amounted to him wanting to put in place a marriage of convenience because it suited him. The most dangerous mistake she could ever make would be to think that there wasn't a fist of steel within the velvet glove.

Cesar reined in his patience with difficulty.

'No. No, I wouldn't want to do that,' he said curtly. He looked away, then back down at her. 'You have all my numbers. Call me, okay?'

Jude had no intention of calling Cesar. She could recognise that there was a thin line between what she saw as making the best of her situation and digging a hole for herself. It could become far too easy to develop a dependency on a Cesar who was pushing the boat out with his friendly charm.

In fact, she looked forward to having some time to herself. She would really focus on her work; there were a couple of projects which needed to be completed. She would also visit Freddy and Imogen and remind herself of what a union between two people should be like because she couldn't afford to be lulled into thinking that what she and Cesar shared was a viable basis for anything more than a couple who would be sharing the upbringing of a child.

What Jude hadn't expected was to return to the house the following Thursday afternoon and have to deal with the unthinkable, the one thing which neither she nor Cesar had factored into the equation.

It was only a couple of spots of blood but at that point in time the bottom seemed to drop out of her world.

Outside, it was a glorious day. She had enjoyed her meeting with the young couple who had been impressed with her designs and she had driven back to the house in an upbeat mood, already looking forward to the distraction of loads of work after the baby was born, which would keep her mind preoccupied. She had concluded that a preoccupied mind was a sure-fire remedy to the daunting prospect of dealing with Cesar.

She could feel the slow swell of panic rising inside her like a destructive tide.

Should she remain where she was? Sit very still and hope that the bleeding stopped? She tried to remember what she had read about unexpected bleeding during pregnancy but her thoughts were all over the place. She was scared to check and terrified by the sickening possibility that she might lose the baby.

And she didn't want to call Cesar.

Her words were stumbling over one another when she eventually mustered all her courage and phoned her doctor. It was probably nothing to worry about, he said…*nothing to worry about!*…but, to be on the safe side, she should go to the hospital…he would phone ahead so that they knew to expect her… *Safe side? Hospital?*

Every word sounded like a death knell to the child growing inside her.

Jude wasn't sure how she managed to have sufficient wits

about her to call a taxi to take her to the hospital, or how she managed to circumnavigate the endless signposted corridors leading to the hundreds of different specialised wards, arriving at the right one, and all this done without breaking down and sobbing.

At some point during the anxious, convoluted journey, she had phoned Imogen and told her what was happening but keeping it light and repeating the doctor's refrain, not a single word of which she actually believed.

'No need to worry Cesar,' she said. 'He's only just back in the country. Very busy. Silly to get him worried for nothing…'

She had given herself stern lectures, had done her damnedest to protect herself from the heartache of being with the man she loved who did not return her love, had laid down the ground rules for dealing with his presence in her life for years to come. She had envisaged a time when he might tell her that he was involved with someone else, had fallen in love against all odds, had finally put the ghost of his wife to rest because he had met someone to whom he was willing to give his heart. And that, unlike all those conveniences the vast reserves of Caretti money could buy, was priceless.

All told, she had recreated a thousand scenarios in her head and all of them had been based on the assumption that they would be sharing a child.

She hadn't imagined a future *without* Cesar's child. She was young, her pregnancy had been straightforward. Not once had she worried about the technicalities of her body doing what it was supposed to do and taking this pregnancy to full term.

Now she was having to contemplate another future and it was one in which Cesar would have nothing to do with her because there would be no need, no duty to fulfil. He wouldn't need to be friendly, witty, attentive. He wouldn't want to have her in a house that was conveniently located so that he could have quick access to her.

True to his word, her doctor had telephoned the hospital in advance of her arrival and she was shown immediately to a bed in the maternity unit to await a scan.

As before, the usual soothing platitudes were rolled out. Jude nodded and pretended to believe them.

She underwent an examination, ignored what her consultant said about not worrying and was taken to have an ultrasound scan.

She wished that Cesar was with her. Then she imagined his face if everything started going wrong and realised that it was a blessing that he wasn't. For the first time it was brought home to her with remorseless clarity just how fragile their relationship was and just how weak she had been in allowing him to take over her life.

Her heart was beating like a hammer as she lay on the narrow bed in the darkened scan room and watched the monitor as the sonographer studied her baby. She was mesmerised by the detail she could see moving. Everything, she was told soothingly, was fine.

Jude realised that nothing was fine. This scare had been gifted to her as a learning curve. She had become complacent. She had fallen victim to her own fanciful notions. What was the point in giving yourself stern lectures and then going out and doing just the opposite? She had allowed herself to set up home in a bubble, won over by a few smiles and kindly gestures.

Besides, the doctors said that everything looked fine. They had also told her that she needed complete bed rest and had been vague when quizzed about worst-case scenarios, telling her that she shouldn't fill her head with nonsense but that she should just take it easy.

With her imagination now doing a merry jig in her head, however, Jude was managing to convince herself that the baby she was so desperate to have, the baby she had foolishly taken for granted, was a vulnerable life held in the balance, its future out of her control.

Changes would have to be made. What she and Cesar shared was a business arrangement and she had stupidly allowed herself to forget that.

Put aside the rose-tinted specs for a minute, she thought relentlessly, and what did she see? Someone keeping her sweet for the time being because it suited him.

What had he been doing, for instance, while he had been away? Cesar Caretti wasn't the average male. He was the stupendously sexy, immensely rich and powerful head of an empire. A man who was well aware of his sex appeal and had never dated anyone who hadn't resembled a model from a glossy magazine. In fact, he had probably dated a fair few *models from glossy magazines*. So was it really likely that he had been to New York and contented himself with business dinners and work? With no play on the side? Especially when he was no longer interested in *her* from a sexual point of view?

Unanswered questions grew in her head, proliferating and twisting themselves around her mind like ivy.

Of course, she would have to see him some time, probably when she was released from the hospital, where she had been advised to stay overnight so that they could monitor her vitals. The bleeding had stopped and, while her level of panic was now receding, her head seemed to have cleared.

She was feeling quite pleased with herself when she finally drifted off to sleep to the sound of trolleys being wheeled outside the little room into which she had been put.

She woke up to the sound of someone in her room, the

quiet pad of footsteps and then the scraping of a chair as it was pulled close to the bed.

Jude knew who it was without opening her eyes. It seemed that something about Cesar could send her antennae onto full alert even when she wasn't actually looking at him.

'How did you know I was here?' She reluctantly opened her eyes and was startled to find him sitting closer to her than she had thought.

'Imogen told me. Why the hell didn't you call me yourself?'

'I didn't see the need.'

Cesar controlled the temptation to explode. He had already had a word with her consultant and been told that everything appeared to be fine but that she should take it easy, at least for the next few weeks. Shouting was just going to stress her out.

'You didn't see the need.'

'No. And Imogen shouldn't have called you. In fact, I asked her not to. You've been away and the last thing I wanted was for you to rush here when you probably had work commitments.' She kept her voice as businesslike as possible. 'It was just a scare, as a matter of fact.'

'I think I have a right to know when you have *a scare*.'

Before, she thought bitterly, she would have subconsciously construed that as a thoughtful gesture that included *her*. It would have given her a warm, tingly feeling and she might have smiled at him and confided how worried she had been. She might even, depending on how much that warm, tingly feeling was, have mentioned that she was glad to see him. He would have taken her back to the house and used that gentle, concerned, friendly voice on her and she would have deluded herself into thinking that she meant something more important than just an incubator for his child. Not now.

'Hopefully, there won't be another,' she said politely and Cesar frowned at her.

'What's the matter?'

'What do you mean?'

'When I left you, you were sunny and upbeat. Is this change of mood because you're worried? The consultant said that there's no need to worry. Actually, the last thing you want to do is get stressed out.'

Because stress might affect the baby. I couldn't give a damn about your welfare!

'Of course.'

'You have to rest. No more working round the clock on fool projects. From now on, you'll put your feet up and listen to what the consultant said. I'll get a housekeeper in. Someone to cook, clean and run whatever errands you want her to run. There'll be no need for you to lift a finger.'

'They're not fool projects.'

'You'll do as I say,' Cesar grated. There was no point pussyfooting round her sensibilities. 'Your good health is the baby's good health, it's as simple as that.' He didn't know what kind of mood she was in but he wasn't best pleased with it. He had rushed to the hospital, worried out of his mind, and that cool voice of hers was getting on his nerves.

Simple as that. It always had been.

'Don't even think about telling me that you can do without a housekeeper,' he said, forestalling any possible idiot objection to this particular ground rule.

'I wasn't. I'm not stupid, Cesar. I realise that I'll need help around the house and I won't be driving out for any more of my *fool projects*, as you call them. At least not for the moment.' She remembered when Imogen had been rushed into hospital. The stricken look on Freddy's face when she'd seen him. That look had been all about love. In that moment she had known that he would have given up everything for Imogen, would have done anything for her.

Cesar's worry was reserved solely for the child she was carrying.

'I'm tired now,' she told him abruptly. 'It's been a long day and I want to go back to sleep.'

'You'll need some clothes.'

Jude hadn't given that a moment's thought. She was still in the hospital gown they had provided. She shrugged and nodded.

'Tell me what you want and I'll bring them.'

'There's really no need to trouble yourself, Cesar. Your driver can fetch what I need.' She stifled a yawn.

'Don't be absurd.' Cesar thought of his driver rifling through her underwear and he scowled with distaste. It was worse than unacceptable. It was obscene. 'I'll get what you need and I'll make sure that a housekeeper is in place by the time you get back to the house. In fact, I'll get my secretary working on that immediately.' He flipped open his cellphone and Jude listened as he gave orders. Orders that would be obeyed without question and handled with a level of efficiency that a high salary guaranteed. His voice was crisp, the voice of a man who knew that when he gave orders, they were obeyed. His secretary was *paid* to obey them.

He had used different tactics on her, though, but the net result was the same. He had given his orders, orders cloaked with smiles and concern, and she had obeyed them. She had even been paid, in a manner of speaking, because where was she living? In a house he had chosen in an area he had picked for reasons that suited him. The only fly he had found in the ointment had been her refusal to marry him, which would have legitimised his baby, but in every other respect he had persuaded her into the corner he had wanted and she had put up very little resistance.

But that scare had reminded her that she was essentially disposable and it was time she sat up and took notice of the fact before she found herself carried too far downstream on the current to ever get back to safe shores.

CHAPTER TEN

I'VE been doing some thinking...

Jude was back at the house and Cesar was on his way. The housekeeper had been employed in record time, had already cleaned the house for Jude's return and had now been dispatched to the supermarket with a list of food items to buy. This so that the house could be empty when Cesar arrived.

She looked in the mirror and carried on with the speech she had rehearsed. She'd been doing some thinking and, first of all, wanted to make sure that the correct documents were signed so that the house which he had bought was in his name. That would establish the tenor of the conversation straight away.

Thereafter, it would be easier to maintain a grip on her emotions, especially when she moved onto the thornier subject of the personal boundaries which needed to exist between them. Of course he would tell her that no boundaries had been crossed, that they were conducting a civilised, adult and perfectly amicable relationship because it would make things easier when it came to jointly caring for their child. She had her answer to that one all worked out. Dinners out went beyond *being friendly* and she wouldn't be put in a position of being *under his thumb*, a single woman to all intents and purposes but one with her life controlled by him. She would raise the issue of what would happen when one of them found a partner, someone meaningful with whom to share their life. Basically, she would let him know, in not so many words, that he was a bystander in her life when it came to her emotions.

Looking at her reflection as she applied some mascara, she wondered what this fictional character, destined to appear at some point on the horizon, would be like. Would she even recognise him as a possibility when her head was so full of Cesar? Even if he was carrying a placard which said *Look No Further, I'm The Man Of Your Dreams*? No one seemed to match up to Cesar. He was so much larger than life that, alongside him, all other men faded into the background. He had burst into her life and had dominated it and she had swooned and fallen in love like a tragic heroine from a Victorian novel.

She made a little grimace at herself and then walked through to the sitting room. From the sofa, she could look out onto the back garden and right now it was bathed in sunshine.

She heard the front door open and knew it was Cesar before he stepped into the sitting room. Those wretched antennae again! Gorgeous, sexy, incredible Cesar in a pair of cream trousers and a rugby shirt which, he'd explained to her some time in a past that now seemed like another lifetime, was a leftover from his university days when he'd been captain of the rugby team.

Jude felt her heart give its usual little flip.

'Obeying doctor's orders,' he said approvingly. 'Good.' He sat down on the chair facing her and crossed his legs. She'd told him to come at four and he'd spent the last three hours edgily aware that he was looking at his watch way too often and wondering why she had told him a specific time when before she had been happy enough for him to pole over whenever he felt like it.

'How are you feeling?'

'Fine. Thank you.'

Fine? Thank you? That same politeness fringed with just a touch of frost. Or was that just his imagination playing tricks on him?

'And the housekeeper? Working out all right? Where is she, anyway?'

'Annie's working out fine and she's at the supermarket right now. I asked her to go because…I really think we need to talk…'

Cesar had no trouble in recognising that tone of voice. He had used it himself in the past, usually on women whose role in his life had gone beyond their sell-by date. Then he would take them out for an expensive meal and over liqueurs would tell them that they *needed to talk*…

'Talk on.'

Jude noticed that the easy smile had left his face. In its place was that shuttered expression which had once chilled her to the bone. 'I…I did a lot of thinking yesterday, Cesar. When I thought that…well, when I thought the worst…and I realise that we really need to sort out one or two details…' She cleared her throat and waited for him to say something.

'What details?' Cesar eventually asked.

'This house, for instance.'

'Is in my name. As you asked.'

'Good.' His dark, watchful eyes were unsettling, making her stumble over the brisk, no nonsense tone she had planned on using. 'And…and we need to discuss what happens if and when either of us meets someone else.'

'Are you telling me that there's someone else?'

'Of course not! Look at me, Cesar. I'm pregnant!'

Of course there wasn't anyone else. It had been a ridiculous question but he had found himself asking it anyway.

'But there might be. One day. Just as there might be for you.' She half hoped that he would deny such a preposterous thing but naturally no such denial was forthcoming and why should it be? He had offered her marriage, had told her that she was eligible for money, as if she were an employee who was worthy of a pay rise after a satisfactory probationary period. He had never said anything about fidelity. She gave voice to something that was only now occurring to her.

'Why did you ask me to marry you, Cesar?'

'Not this again!'

'I know you're a traditionalist. I know you don't like the thought of having a baby born out of wedlock. But was it also because you didn't want any other man on the scene? Muddying the waters with the upbringing of your child?'

'That thought never crossed my mind!' But Cesar flushed. Had it crossed his mind? Even subconsciously? Was that why he felt more comfortable with her living closer to him? Because he could keep an eye on her? He didn't like the thought of being possessive. He had never been a possessive man. Indeed, had never felt the need to know the whereabouts of any of the women he had dated in the past, although he had always known that none of them would have thought about straying. Even with Marisol…yes, he had been protective. She had been very feminine and very helpless, had needed his protection…but possessive?

'Where is this going?' he asked harshly. 'Have I not complied with every request you've made?' She had been fine a few days previously. What had changed?

Jude saw that dark flush that had stained his high, aristocratic cheekbones when she had asked him about his reasons for proposing to her and knew, with a sinking heart, that she had hit a tender nerve. He would tether her to him, would make it impossible for her to ever find anyone else because he would have no other man interfere in his child's life. It was a game played by his rules and only his rules.

'I'm laying down a few ground rules,' she told him steadily. 'I thought that I was going to lose the baby. In fact, right now I'm taking nothing for granted.'

'Has the consultant said anything to you that he kept from me?' Cesar demanded, frowning. 'If he has, there will be hell to pay!'

'This doesn't have anything to do with the baby.' Jude looked away. She didn't want to see his expression close over. 'This has to do with me. Actually, with *us*.'

'If we're talking about *us*, I thought we were getting along just fine until I came back to England to discover a black cloud hanging over you.'

'We *are* getting along just fine,' Jude told him. 'But I think it's important to remember that we're not *friends*. We're two people who made a mistake by sleeping together and getting more than either of us bargained for. Let's not forget that we wouldn't, actually, be here having any sort of conversation if I hadn't discovered that I was pregnant. I appreciate all that you've done...'

'Will you stop talking to me as though I'm a stranger!'

'And stop shouting at me in my own house!'

'But it's *not* your own house, is it?'

There was a tense, electric silence and then Jude said slowly, the colour draining from her face, 'Is that it, Cesar? Your house and therefore I have to abide by your rules? Toe the line because you've paid for the roof over my head? The roof, incidentally, that I don't remember *asking* for?'

'This is ridiculous!' Cesar said fiercely.

'No, it's not!' She thought of his trip to swinging New York. 'Okay, here's a question. How would you feel if I *did* meet someone down the line—someone I wanted to play a big part in my life? Someone who would inevitably come into contact with our child? Have an influence over him or her? Would that be all right with you? Or would I have to abide by *your* rules so long as I'm living in a house *you* paid for?'

Cesar dearly wanted to inform her that *she* could do as she damn well wanted to do, just so long as *his* child was kept out of it, but images of her with another man made him clench his jaw in fury.

'Don't worry about answering that, Cesar. I know the answer from your silence. You…you think you can do whatever you want while I stay in the house you paid for doing motherly things!'

'Do whatever I want?'

Jude realised that somewhere along the line her cool, calm, mature speech had gone down the pan. Now, she felt like bursting into tears.

'I mean, what did you get up to in New York?' she was appalled to hear herself ask, especially when he was looking at her as though she had taken leave of her senses. 'Not that I care. I'm just saying that to *prove a point*. You are free to do whatever you want, and I expect to be free to do whatever *I* want as well.'

'So let me get this straight,' Cesar said tightly. 'If I told you that I went to New York, met up with an old flame and spent three very sexy nights with her, you wouldn't be bothered.'

'Did you?'

'At the risk of flying in the face of all your preconceptions, no, I didn't.'

'That's not to say that you won't some time in the future,' Jude goaded him, relieved to death by what he had said but already bleakly contemplating a time when his answer would be different and hating herself for knowing that she would always care enough to ask and to be hurt.

'And, of course, if I did, you wouldn't try to stop me.'

'What would be the point? You're a free man, Cesar. Even if we got married, you would still be a free man and there'd be nothing I could ever do to hold you back.'

Cesar thought that once he had been a free man and any hint of a woman trying to tame him would have signalled the immediate end to a relationship. But did a free man lose track of work because his mind was too taken up with one very stubborn, very frustrating woman with short dark hair and a line of conversation that had absolutely no respect for his barriers? And did a free man count the hours until he could see the one woman who consumed his every waking moment? He found it hard to remember when he had last been a free man.

Now she was talking about Marisol, telling him what might have been true once upon a time. He held up one hand, cutting her off in mid-rant and waited until she had subsided into silence.

'Everything you're telling me is true,' he admitted roughly, leaning forward, elbows on his knees. He ran his fingers through his hair, a gesture with which Jude had become so familiar that it brought a lump to her throat.

'I loved Marisol. Hell, we were so young and had so little time together. Too little time to really find out each other's faults and yes, I put her on a pedestal.' His coal-black eyes tangled with hers.

Jude wanted to put her hand over his beautiful mouth

because she didn't want him confirming everything she had just said. She realised that in all her mentally rehearsed speeches, he had largely been a silent listener.

'She was…compliant, soft, subservient…'

'I know. I think you've told me this before. She was everything I'm not.'

Cesar nodded in confirmation. 'Which makes me wonder whether we were ever really suited.'

'What?' She raised her head and focused her wide brown eyes on his face.

He felt a giddy, strange sensation, as though he were standing on the edge of an abyss, looking down.

'I always thought that sweet and subservient was what I wanted until I met a headstrong, mouthy, argumentative woman who had the nerve to question everything I did and said and thought.'

Jude found that she was holding her breath, wondering whether she was hearing properly, but the expression on his face told her that she was. He looked oddly vulnerable. It wasn't an expression she had ever seen before. She wanted to reach out and go across to him, sit on his lap, stroke his face, but she also didn't want the spell to end.

'When I left your cottage, I really thought that I could return to London, that my life would pick up where it had left off. I was accustomed to women being transient. Sure, my ego was hurting because you'd sent me on my bike when I wanted to prolong what we had, but I told myself that it was for the best. Thing is, I couldn't get you out of my mind.'

'You couldn't?'

Cesar shook his head wryly.

'That's probably because…you know…the sex thing…wanting the one thing you thought you couldn't have…'

CATHY WILLIAMS   179

'Are you fishing, by any chance?'

Jude grinned reluctantly at him. 'Sort of.'

'Fishing for what?'

She shrugged and watched as he covered the distance separating them, until he was sitting on the sofa by her so that she was squashed to one side to accommodate his big body. Very happily squashed because she had missed him being close to her, feeling the warmth of his body. He was so vibrant, so *aggressively alive* and he made her feel the same. Without him, she was a shadow, lacking definition.

'It's not the sex thing. In fact, it's nothing to do with sex. Sure, when I think about you, I feel horny, but I also feel…incomplete. I guess what I'm trying to say is that I love you. I can't think of you with any other man and it's got nothing to do with wanting to protect my kid from someone else's influence. It's got to do with something a hell of a lot more primitive than that. I think it's called jealousy.'

'You're *jealous*!' She smiled a wide sunny smile and took one of his hands in hers, liking the way he played with her fingers.

'I think it's a side effect of being in love.'

'And I love you, too.'

'If you love me, why won't you make an honest man of me and marry me?'

'I was waiting, Cesar, for you to say the right words and now you have. I'll marry you whenever you want me to.'

They were married six weeks later in a very small, very intimate ceremony with just family and close friends. By this time Jude was back on her feet, although all work commitments that involved her driving were put on hold.

Like Imogen, there was no honeymoon and, like Imogen, Jude didn't mind in the slightest. She was so happy that she wouldn't have minded if she never left the country. She was content to be wherever Cesar was, even if that meant staying put in her little house with him, eating meals in and looking after the garden, for he had moved out of his apartment. She no longer recognised him for the workaholic she had first met and he had even been making noises about moving farther away from London when the time was right. For a man who had once considered Kent the back of beyond, this was a big step.

After what turned out to be an uneventful pregnancy, Olivia Caretti was born on a bright, sunny afternoon and seemed determined to compensate for all the stress that had surrounded her conception by coming into the world with very little fuss.

She had a head of very dark hair and was a very sweet-tempered baby, calmly accepting the doting attention that was lavished on her with happy gurgles. She was christened several weeks after her birth. Imogen was her godmother and Freddy her godfather, with strict instructions never to allow her near any clubs, including his, which was fast developing a reputation as the best jazz club in the county.

Life could not have been happier.

And now, with winter fast approaching and Christmas just around the corner, the air was fragrant with the anticipation of buying their first Christmas tree together.

'The first of many,' Cesar had told her the night before, after they had made passionate love and had lain in bed, just talking while their baby slept in the room next door. 'And, pretty soon, I'm hoping you give me a reason for us to move a little farther out into something a little bigger…'

'What kind of reason?' Jude had known exactly what he was talking about and for the past five hours she had been waiting for just the right, special moment to tell him what she had to tell him.

'What kind do you think, Mrs Caretti?'

'Well, now, funny you should say that because we might have a very good reason in...oh...eight and a half months time. I did a test this morning, Mr Caretti, and it seems that you're as virile as you keep telling me, after all...'

* * * * *

*Celebrate 60 years of pure reading pleasure
with Harlequin®!*

*Harlequin Presents® is proud to introduce
its gripping new miniseries,*
THE ROYAL HOUSE OF KAREDES.
*An exquisite coronation diamond, split as a symbol of a
warring royal family's feud, is missing! But whoever
reunites the diamond halves will rule all….*

*Welcome to eight brand-new titles that unfold to reveal the
stories of kings and queens, princes and princesses torn
apart by pride and power, but finally reunited by love.*

Step into the world of Karedes with
BILLIONAIRE PRINCE, PREGNANT MISTRESS
Available July 2009
from Harlequin Presents®.

ALEXANDROS KAREDES, SNOW DUSTING the shoulders of his leather jacket and glittering like jewels in his dark hair, stood at the door. Maria felt the blood drain from her head.

"Good evening, Ms. Santos."

His voice was as she remembered it. Deep. Husky. Perfect English, but with the faintest hint of a Greek accent. And cold, as cold as it had been that awful morning she would never forget, when he'd accused her of horrible things, called her terrible names....

"Aren't you going to ask me in?"

She fought for composure. Last time they'd faced each other, they'd been on his turf. Now they were on hers. She was in command here, and that meant everything.

"There's a sign on the door downstairs," she said, her tone every bit as frigid as his. "It says, 'No soliciting or vagrants.'"

His lips drew back in a wolfish grin. "Very amusing."

"What do you want, Prince Alexandros?"

A tight smile eased across his mouth and it killed her that even now, knowing he was a vicious, arrogant man, she couldn't help but notice what a handsome mouth it was. Chiseled.

Generous. Beautiful, like the rest of him, which made him living proof that beauty could, indeed, be only skin deep.

"Such formality, Maria. You were hardly so proper the last time we were together."

She knew his choice of words was deliberate. She felt her face heat; she couldn't help that but she damned well didn't have to let him lure her into a verbal sparring match.

"I'll ask you once more, your highness. What do you want?"

"Ask me in and I'll tell you."

"I have no intention of asking you in. Tell me why you're here or don't. It's your choice, just as it will be my choice to shut the door in your face."

He laughed. It infuriated her but she could hardly blame him. He was tall—six two, six three—and though he stood with one shoulder leaning against the door frame, hands tucked casually into the pockets of the jacket, his pose was deceptive. He was strong, with the leanly muscled body of a well-trained athlete.

She remembered his body with painful clarity. The feel of him under her hands. The power of him moving over her. The taste of him on her tongue.

Suddenly, he straightened, his laughter gone. "I have not come this distance to stand in your doorway," he said coldly, "and I am not going to leave until I am ready to do so. I suggest you stand aside and stop behaving like a petulant child."

A petulant child? Was that what he thought? This man who had spent hours making love to her and had then accused her of—of trading her body for profit?

Except it had not been love, it had been sex. And the sooner she got rid of him, the better.

She let go of the doorknob and stepped aside. "You have five minutes."

He strolled past her, bringing cold air and the scent of the night with him. She swung toward him, arms folded. He reached past her, pushed the door closed, then folded his arms, too. She wanted to open the door again but she'd be damned if she was going to get into a who's-in-charge-here argument with him. She was in charge, and he would surely see a tussle over the ground rules as a sign of weakness.

Instead, she looked past him at the big clock above her work table.

"Ten seconds gone," she said briskly. "You're wasting time, your highness."

"What I have to say will take longer than five minutes."

"Then you'll just have to learn to economize. More than five minutes, I'll call the police."

Instantly, his hand was wrapped around her wrist. He tugged her toward him, his dark-chocolate eyes almost black with anger.

"You do that and I'll tell every tabloid shark I can contact about how Maria Santos tried to buy a five-hundred-thousand-dollar commission by seducing a prince." He smiled thinly. "They'll lap it up."

* * * * *

What will it take for this billionaire prince to realize he's falling in love with his mistress…?
Look for
BILLIONAIRE PRINCE, PREGNANT MISTRESS
by Sandra Marton
Available July 2009 from Harlequin Presents®.

We'll be spotlighting a different series every month
throughout 2009 to celebrate our 60th anniversary.

Look for Harlequin® Presents in July!

TWO CROWNS, TWO ISLANDS, ONE LEGACY
A royal family, torn apart by pride and its lust for
power, reunited by purity and passion

Step into the world of Karedes
beginning this July with

BILLIONAIRE PRINCE,
PREGNANT MISTRESS
by
Sandra Marton

Eight volumes to collect and treasure!

FORCED TO MARRY

Wives for the taking!

Once these men put a diamond ring on their bride's
finger, there's no going back….

Wedlocked and willful, these wives will get a
wedding night they'll never forget!

REQUEST YOUR FREE BOOKS!

HARLEQUIN *Presents* ®

PASSION GUARANTEED SEDUCTION

2 FREE NOVELS
PLUS 2
FREE GIFTS!

YES! Please send me 2 FREE Harlequin Presents® novels and my 2 FREE gifts (gifts are worth about $10). After receiving them, if I don't wish to receive any more books, I can return the shipping statement marked "cancel". If I don't cancel, I will receive 6 brand-new novels every month and be billed just $4.05 per book in the U.S. or $4.74 per book in Canada. That's a savings of close to 15% off the cover price! It's quite a bargain! Shipping and handling is just 25¢ per book*. I understand that accepting the 2 free books and gifts places me under no obligation to buy anything. I can always return a shipment and cancel at any time. Even if I never buy another book, the two free books and gifts are mine to keep forever.

106 HDN ERRW 306 HDN ERRL

Name	(PLEASE PRINT)
Address	Apt. #
City	State/Prov.	Zip/Postal Code

Signature (if under 18, a parent or guardian must sign)

Mail to the **Harlequin Reader Service:**
IN U.S.A.: P.O. Box 1867, Buffalo, NY 14240-1867
IN CANADA: P.O. Box 609, Fort Erie, Ontario L2A 5X3

Not valid to current subscribers of Harlequin Presents books.

Are you a current subscriber of Harlequin Presents books and want to receive the larger-print edition? Call 1-800-873-8635 today!

* Terms and prices subject to change without notice. Prices do not include applicable taxes. Sales tax applicable in N.Y. Canadian residents will be charged applicable provincial taxes and GST. Offer not valid in Quebec. This offer is limited to one order per household. All orders subject to approval. Credit or debit balances in a customer's account(s) may be offset by any other outstanding balance owed by or to the customer. Please allow 4 to 6 weeks for delivery. Offer available while quantities last.

Your Privacy: Harlequin Books is committed to protecting your privacy. Our Privacy Policy is available online at www.eHarlequin.com or upon request from the Reader Service. From time to time we make our lists of customers available to reputable third parties who may have a product or service of interest to you. If you would prefer we not share your name and address, please check here. ☐

HP09

HARLEQUIN *Presents*

TWO CROWNS, TWO ISLANDS, ONE LEGACY

A royal family, torn apart by pride and its lust for power, reunited by purity and passion

THE ROYAL HOUSE *of* KAREDES

coming in 2009

BILLIONAIRE PRINCE, PREGNANT MISTRESS
by Sandra Marton, July

THE PLAYBOY SHEIKH'S VIRGIN STABLE-GIRL
by Sharon Kendrick, August

THE PRINCE'S CAPTIVE WIFE
by Marion Lennox, September

THE SHEIKH'S FORBIDDEN VIRGIN
by Kate Hewitt, October

THE GREEK BILLIONAIRE'S
INNOCENT PRINCESS
by Chantelle Shaw, November

THE FUTURE KING'S LOVE-CHILD
by Melanie Milburne, December

RUTHLESS BOSS, ROYAL MISTRESS
by Natalie Anderson, January

THE DESERT KING'S HOUSEKEEPER BRIDE
by Carol Marinelli, February

8 volumes to collect and treasure!

HARLEQUIN *Presents*

International Billionaires

Life is a game of power and pleasure.
And these men play to win!

THE SHEIKH'S LOVE-CHILD
by *Kate Hewitt*

When Lucy arrives in the desert kingdom of Biryal,
Sheikh Khaled's eyes are blacker and harder than
before. But Lucy and the sheikh are inextricably
bound forever—for he is the father of her son....

Book #2838

Available July 2009